Other books by Sherrie DeMorrow:

*The Knight and Daye series*:

Knight and Daye
Cloud of Dreams
The Elder Rose
All The Land
The Little Bird
Beyond the Land
A Little Princess
Romancing the West
The Silver Millions
The Painted Chapel
A Hound's Desire
Space of Things

*The Young Dr Huer series*:

A Beginners Realm
Flight Into Space
My Brother, Draconian
The Widowed Advent

# THE WIDOWED ADVENT

## BY

## SHERRIE DEMORROW

Published 2021 by

Lightning Source (UK) Ltd
Chapter House,
Pitfield,
Kiln Farm,
Milton Keynes
MK11 3LW,
UK



Cover Art Design by Sam Wall

*In Memory of Tim
With love*

PREFACE and AUTHOR'S NOTE

Please be advised this novel is the conclusion of a backstory of the character of Dr Elias Huer of the *Buck Rogers in the 25th Century* series, old and new, but I am basing it on the television series that aired from 1979-81. However, the events in this story PREDATE the television series, and cover Dr Huer's younger years, up until the series itself. Then the story ends.

I did write to gain permission from Universal to use this character, but I got no answer. Hence, I am writing these new series of books in loving tribute to the man who portrayed Dr Huer in the television version, Tim O'Connor. Tim has made appearances in several of my books, re-imagining a character for him in the *Knight and Daye* series that I just completed. This story does draw from those books, to put a cohesive backstory to the Dr Huer character. I want to give the man more than just a 'desk job'. I want to see what his early years were like, for example: what he thought, how he lived. Was the 25th century all that it was cracked up to be, as it was shown on television? Why did Dr Huer seem so sad? I want to see the good doctor in action, like Buck Rogers from the previous shows. A lot of the time, the doctor was so dead-pan serious, it made me wonder. An actor of the older generation would display vast amounts of seriousness to a role that was expected to be serious. However, the portrayal was so good, it made the character dull and boring. I do not believe (and I refuse to believe) that he was really like that. There is much to explore, and to examine the nature of Dr Huer is an excellent example of fandom, indeed.

Some place names and characters given are based on the television series (like New Chicago, or Anarchia, Kane and Twiki); acknow-ledgements for this had been made previously.

Other characters, mentioned or otherwise, are fictional and loosely based on people known of by the author, or from the previous *Knight and Daye* series. Any personalities referred to herein are used (again), in loving tribute.

If there is anything amiss, please write to the publisher, and it shall be corrected.

# CHAPTER I

Every beginning has an ending, and I firmly believed I faced mine. Cindy was a sweet, good woman with a childish streak about her that raced through many games, back in the day. In our day, she was my wife. I married her to better myself. What was worse was that my best friend in childhood, Antssarah Kane, saw fit to shoot her down. I was very sore and angry that he would do such a thing, and I never forgave him afterwards. I began to hate Dracos for all its so-called power and self-seeking glory. What had been an exploration in space, with a quiet flirtation with the wife and a brotherly visit, turned into a nightmare of horrible proportions. The sadness that came over me had stayed, as Dr Wildock and his staff wheeled her down that corridor, and turned a corner that led to unknown results. I hoped they would do all it took to save my beautiful lass, and the growing baby inside her.

*Oh God, now I'm sounding like Silage.*

*Silage.* He had his problems too, and deep regrets, though he didn't tell me everything, IF there was anything to tell. Forgiving him would be challenging, as it was he who went to Dracos and got too involved, which put us into this mess in the first place. Deep down, I really wanted to check up on him, just to see if he was okay. It was a personal gesture, nothing more; just concern for my wayward brother. It pained me to see how he'd changed since being on Dracos, and his giving himself away to such a barbaric society. The Kane brothers, maybe; their dark looks gave way to darker intentions. They served their Emperor and my Cindy paid the price. My little flower of Anarchia, gone; *as if there were flowers in Anarchia!* I knew it was a form of civilisation, but an instinct of lethal proportions lurked beneath, if you knew where to look. And I did, regrettably so.

Suddenly, I heard my name called.

'Elias.'

There it was again; it was Pemur.

He saw me and Silage sitting in the waiting area, and approached slowly.  Lt Selina Cayley went off somewhere, leaving me alone with my brother.  I spoke no words to him.  I wasn't in the mood.  My countenance showed a crestfallen man, with the ridges falling into the ocean.

'Elias,' he put his hand on my shoulder, 'You may go in now to see her.'

Dumbly I asked, 'How is she?'

'Under the circumstances, comfortable,' he muttered, 'But I think you should look in on her yourself.'

'Thanks,' I grinned meekly, getting up for the inevitable.

I walked into the white lit room with a red border in the middle.  The instruments were alive with beeps and bonks, and various drones had been plugged in to save her.  Cindy was riddled with wires, it seemed and it looked like she herself would get up somehow, like an ancient scientific experimentation. It was a far cry from the science that I knew of.

I looked down upon her, all in that tangled mess, with a respirator attachment.  I then looked at Pemur and made a weak attempt in dismissing him.

'Surely you have Directorate duties.'

With the air ringing silently in his lapels, he turned to me. 'That's what little lady lieutenants are for. I've had Cayley take over, so I can be with you.'

'Thanks,' I added meekly, still indicating the wish to be alone with her.

*It appeared that Pemur wasn't so shallow after all.*

'I'll wait outside for you, Elias.'

He walked away and left me to my wire-attached wife. When I cried over her, a drone called out to me, 'Hey, you'll short circuit everything here. Keep your tears to yourself!'

'Sorry,' I said, wiping my eyes with a shirtsleeve, astonished at his in-sensitivity.

Cindy awoke for a bit, but very dazed and tired. 'Elias.'

'My love,' I kissed her hand and held it for some time. 'You don't know what this means to me.'

'I do. I've given you hope for something,' she said, 'But it won't be long now. You'll be that flashy scientist sooner than you think; you already scouted the stars.'

'No, no, you've got to come back, you've got to. I love you so much.'

'Elias… I...'

'Yes?'

'I really love you, too. Take care my dear; your dumb-fuck days are coming soon. Even if I don't get out of this, I'll always love you, E..li...as...'

Her hand went limp and lifeless. She drifted like driftwood upon the sea; I could feel her floating, somewhere, into the beyond.

'Cindy, no,' I screamed.

The charts let off a small beep and a horizontal indicator streaked across the monitor. Medicine in the 25th century was not crude by any means, but not as advanced as people made it out to be. We all had to begin again from the time of the Big Blast, but it took further ingenuity for us to get this far. Problem was, Death still existed.

'No, no,' I continued, opposing fate. 'I won't let you go, Cindy. I don't want you to go.'

I tried one last time to 'save' her; I gripped the screen to change its pulse-line and cried out, with the already elongated line passing ominously by.

'Release the monitor,' another drone commanded me from its station, and with utter disdain, called out, 'She's dead. Tough shit on you, Huer.'

Pemur rushed in and held on to me, as the drone made a rude noise. It was as cruel as raw porridge on the coldest winter day. I wanted to blast that accursed thing out of the room, when the robots in the vicinity alerted the human medics and Dr Wildock came in.

We gave him a few moments for him to check his patient, my wife. He hung his head and announced to us. 'She is gone. I'm sorry Elias.'

'No, no, no,' I firmly protested, hoping the earlier screen-readings were false, and I was hallucinating about the dim news.

'We must be strong now,' Wildock grabbed me and held me still, 'Do you think I hadn't lost patients these days. Look, I know she was your wife. Though the stun itself showed no serious effects, the shot had put her into shock. The emerging child inside her also suffered and was dead on the spot. It was too small to withstand that Draconian weapon.'

'No, no,' I shook my head in disbelief. 'Oh God!'

'Elias,' Pemur came in like a calm mystic, 'Let her go and come with me.'

I screamed a shrill that broke a few other monitors, including Cindy's. *Good, that's what I think of you, Death!*

'Get this disruptive barbaric out of this room,' the drone barked out. 'We cannot handle this apocalyptic emotion.'

'Come on, Huer,' Wildock invited, 'Let's go for a drink.'

I had no choice. My Cindy just lay there, still; the final word uttered was my name. At least she'll go to the beyond, knowing my love for her. I left the room, hunched over and a complete mess.

Silage came up to me. 'Elias, are you alright?'

'She's dead.  Cindy's dead,' I moaned again.

I slumped into a corner, away from everyone.  I breathed heavy and felt so alone.

With equal suffering, my brother then added, 'I'm deeply sorry, Elias.'

'I bet you are,' I sneered back.

'No, it's not what you think,' he explained, 'I admit I liked her to flirtation, but I knew she was your girl.'

'That's not what I saw.'

'Well, believe what you want, but here I am, giving you my condolences.  Take them or leave them,' he said.

'I'm sorry, Silage,' I reached out to hug him.

As brothers, it was very odd for us to even want to be together, but now, we embraced with such grief, it was nothing as I could have imagined.  In a greedy stance, I wanted Cindy for myself, her being my wife and all, but Silage showed genuine care for her.  It was rather kind of him to do so; fighting for honour at this point was meaningless.

# CHAPTER II

So not only had I lost Cindy, I also lost my chance at being a father. A baby would have been so much fun to be with and raise, teaching him or her all the things Dad told me. I knew an embryonic baby could never survive a blast from a Draconian weapon, but *damn, why me?* Cindy and the baby were wheeled past me, into the mortuary room to be prepared for the funeral. *Not another funeral!*

Sobbing, I was still held by Silage, when Pemur approached us.

'Elias, Silas, I give you my deepest sympathies,' he said. 'Let's go to your apartment. We can plan from there.'

'Okay,' I agreed.

We went to the place Cindy and I lived and we all embraced in a brotherly hug, though Pemur, I looked upon as a father. I was just a scientist-to-be, as well as a pilot, with a poor rate beginning. I felt stunned, frightened and extremely unhappy. Silage and Pemur talked amongst themselves, mostly because I didn't want to join in. There was no point now and I wasn't in the mood. They were planning the funeral and I didn't care about the data. The only woman I ever loved had died at the hands of cruel Draconian mastery. My otherwise warm heart remained in this cold frontier of death. My eyes gushed wildly like an atomic waterfall. I personally didn't wish to think on it again, as I continued crying, as my passions yet claimed me. So straight-laced was I, I couldn't see through it. I saw a photo of Cindy and I taken at our wedding. I stared into Cindy's eyes, and they became the stars in the sky.

I started feeling nauseous and excused myself to the bathroom. I closed the door and let loose in the toilet.

Pemur and Silage came to the door to see if I was okay.  Well, I wasn't, but at least the physical discomfort ended.

I walked out.  'Yes, I'm okay.'

'No you're not,' Pemur declared.

My soul felt destroyed, but not by the chill of science. 'Really, I'm alright.'

'No you're not,' Silage chimed in.  'I'll stay with you.'

It would have been good to use science for the saving of Cindy, but even science had its limits.  Yet it had benefits that foreshadowed everything.  There were so many possibilities that soon, I decided to give my life to the cause.  It would have been good to save her, but I felt left out, and I had no one to turn to.  Even Twiki and Theo, who were in the apartment and now reactivated, couldn't console me properly.  None of my friends nor brother could alleviate this mask of despair I felt on my face, since her passing.  I honestly couldn't believe she was gone.  Why, it wasn't too long ago, when she and I were on the bed, having a bit of fun, drinking the naughty fuquwer, celebrating one another like it wasn't tomorrow.  Even the morning of our fateful flight which led us to that stargate, didn't escape my memories, which combed through my fine dark hair, with a satisfactory call at the end.

And why did my best friend, of all people, kill my woman?  *Antsy. What was he thinking?  What was the point of killing Cindy?*  Okay, so I didn't tell the Draconians about the stargate.  *Big deal.*  At least it was still out there to be discovered, if they had the incentive to do so.

The good thing was that I spared a future star system from Draconian tyranny, for now.  It was up to the Draconians to explore it for themselves.  Only then will it matter.

'I'll be going along to the Directorate.  You and Silage stay together, and we will meet later on,' Pemur suggested.

'See ya,' I weakly waved at him.

Silage nodded at him and he walked out. We were alone again.  Two brothers in a small bland apartment.  Bland, because Cindy was no longer with us.

He turned to me. 'How are you doing, Elias?'

'Lousy,' I answered him, 'What else is there? I'm finished and you're still unmarried.'

'Well, at least we got out of there,' he said.

'Why, I thought it was home to you.'

'Not after Antssarah shot your Cindy.'

Well, it was good that Silage was on my side for a change.  He did care, beyond looks.  His early interpretive beginning of his flirtations had turned into a serious concern for me. I truly wanted Cindy, but there was no Cindy.

'We'll be together as a family now,' he continued.

'Fat chance,' I uttered.

I really didn't want him around.  After all we'd been through, it was tough to see it end like this.

The week turned into the next, and I just slumped my way through it. The funeral came and went, and I was listless through that.  The event was a small gathering of Silage, Busdon, Cayley, Twiki, Theo and Pemur.  The preacher at the Church of Inner City Central was pleasant enough, but not in a jovial sense.  He knew it had been awhile since I last attended, and at the moment, I didn't care.  The walls provided some soothing comfort to me, as the preacher didn't want our souls to be destroyed by the cold walls of science.  Or death. *Why should I have faith in love, when that love had been taken away from me, and cast into oblivion?* I looked around the brightly coloured windows. They captured an eyeful that lay dormant for way too long.  They made their way into caring and feeling, making love in the ashes of mankind.

The service had concluded and the casket carrying my beloved was taken to a crematorium.  I cried even more, knowing it was Cindy and our unborn that were sacrificed, *just for a friggin' stargate!*

'Easy, easy son,' the preacher, called Julian, held me up.  'She's okay now.'

'But I am not,' I spat back at him, nearly sick of the false optimism religion provided.  It was also something that made my father bitterly struggle through.

'She's somewhere else now, far away, safe and waiting for you.'

I turned on the old fellow.  'Waiting for me?  To die??'

'No no, sonny,' he explained, his fawn-coloured eyes shining brightly, 'To live.  You now live for her, in her memory, as it were.'

He led me into his office.  Like a fallen sheep, I followed him in and recalled what she said to me before she died, that I would become a scientist and a bore; the latter stated more colourfully.  I left everyone where they were, as they figured this preacher might help me.  They probably went somewhere else for a bite or a drink.  The office was snug, and full of books, with odd scraps of paper flown about, it seemed.  It looked like a wizard's hovel, but more sophisticated for our era.  Shame Silage didn't come with me.  He and this preacher would have tons to talk about and Silage would be gawking at these walls of books.

Julian rifled through some things in a drawer and came up with this beautifully bound, medium sized green book.  It was a Bible.

'I've got many of these, lad,' he said, 'Take this, and put it in your place for comfort and well being.  You read it and you will get through this.'

It was touching for him to tell me this, much less to give me a gift. 'Thank you,' I accepted the gift.  I thumbed through it, and it wasn't anything I hadn't seen before.  Admittedly, I found it to be a cooling balm on my charred soul, when I glanced at the words; this was something least mentioned in my life.  *It wasn't too late to begin again.*

'God be with you, in your house and wherever you go, whatever you study,' Julian blessed me, making the sign of the cross.

I found a piece of his blessing a bit off. 'Whatever I study?'

'You are the son of Elias Huer, Sr.  I remember him.  Good man, kept to himself, mostly lab work, I guess.  Still, I trust you will take after him, so may God reach out to you in your studies.'

I was touched by his guidance and support, and wanted to give him a hug.  The embarrassment factor rose steadily by the minutes.

'Oh, tish, say no more about that,' the preacher reached out to embrace me.

*His sense of the archaic would have turned on Silage.*

'Maybe God sees something special in you, Elias Jr,' he added.

'Yeah,' I mildly agreed. 'Thank you so much.'

I smiled, grasping that green bound Bible, and left the hollow eyed cavern that was Julian's office.  I kept the Bible in the crook of my arm and joined my friends and Silage.

'About time, Elias. You've been with that fellow awhile.' Silage acknowledged the book, 'What've you got there?'

I showed him. 'The preacher gave it to me.  It's a Bible.  You should have seen his office.  You would have loved it.'

'I'm sure I would have,' Silage smiled at me.  'Maybe you'll turn to the ancients.'

'That book will look nice in an office,' Pemur added.

I turned to him. 'Yours?'

'No,' he said, 'Yours.'

*Ha-ha. Imagine me turning to Silage's many inspirations.*

Silage put his arm around me.  'You can find comfort in ready ways. I can help you.'

I looked at him, and walked on.  'We'll see.'

I knew I wasn't being very helpful in supporting his proposal.  I looked at the Bible, and thought about Julian's words of praise and human love. I embraced it for a bit, looking it over when we returned home.  Pity Silage didn't have his books; we could have compared notes.  Yet, I knew these were tales of a different sort, though not unlike the crazy myths of the past.

# CHAPTER III

Sometime later, Silage and I returned to our quarters, and relaxed. Newly housed in the sky-scraper-tall white building of the Director-ate, it had been a long time since we were really 'together' in the same place.  I was touched by his caring for me during the while. Our bond was beginning to show now.  I didn't want to get too close to him though, for fear he may have something else up his sleeve. *But no.  He did not.*  Silage was as clean as he was when we were children, before the mess of mythology began.

'I wish I had my books again,' he lamented.  He went over to a small bookcase full of varied volumes, mostly about science. He then no-ticed that Bible I took home.

Smiling, I asked, 'Found something for yourself?'

'Funny item to see in a stack full of scientific materials, ain't it?'

'Well, there you go. Maybe I am going toward the primitive.'

Silage smiled back at me and perused the volume given to me by Ju-lian, the preacher who officiated Cindy's funeral.  I admitted to my-self he was a nice fellow and I wished the world of happiness for him.  I knew though he would want happiness for the *next* world.

I watched Silage reading, and thought to do some of my own, when a chime rang out.  Silage put the book down and went for the door. Sliding the upper panel, it turned out to be Pemur.

The door was open and Pemur barged in, looking very panicked. 'The Computer Council demands to try you both, Silas and Elias.  They are charging you with treason.'

Surprised looks came over us, and for a change we were on the same side.  Silage dryly noted, 'This is about that stargate, isn't it?'

'No, that's not possible,' I cried.  'I was just trying to get out of there, making some stupid story up to appease the Draconians.'

'I admit I was attempting to get the information from you, Elias, but did not succeed when we saw the Emperor,' Silage concurred, 'You tricked me with a spell.'

'It was for our own good,' I shouted at my zany brother.

Pemur shook his head, for now ignoring the word *spell*.  'Well, you are both in trouble with the Council, at least because you were in enemy territory. They deem you a threat to Earth's safety.'

'The Draconians are not our enemies,' Silage defended, 'They opened up an academic opportunity and we took it.  Many from Earth went to Dracos.'

'Yes, but not many from Earth went exploring and found a stargate, like your brother and his late wife did,' Pemur stated, 'The Council thinks otherwise.  It is very hard to argue with them on such a topic as this.  It is not light material, you know.'

'I agree with you Pemur,' I fought back, raising my voice at him, 'But we had not told them anything.  We were on Dracos, yes, but we would never ever tell them about the stargate, nor had any intentions to.  Not even Cindy, and she lost her life over this.'

Pemur felt deflated about the whole thing.  'I know, Elias, I know. Tell it to the judge.'

'Theo will be your counsel and unfortunately, Dr Ruckus is your opposer,' Pemur added.

Silage uttered, 'That bag of bolts!'

'Bag of bolts or not, you will have to deal with him,' Pemur concluded, 'And no magic tricks, Silas. You see what happens when you deal with things that are misunderstood.'

Silage and I were both reeling from the news still. True, Silage did use magic to try to trick me into getting the stargate information, but I used magic against him, to shut him up. Pemur had a fit when we told him that wizardry was used to get to me, but he didn't believe it. I highly doubted Dr Ruckus would believe it, either, and he was a machine!

Pemur looked hopeful for a moment. 'We could always go through Meg's consoles on *The Ancient Crab*.'

'Meg won't tell you anything,' I explained, 'When we got to the ship, it was completely powered down. I guessed the recharge was complete. When we waylaid that Draconian guard who accompanied us, and got him out of the way, I had to switch the controls on to access Meg again.'

'We will still look anyway,' Pemur said, 'We need to see it for ourselves. Meantime, I will have to put you under arrest for the time being, until your trial.'

We were led out to a vehicle that took us to another hell of a prison; *as if a Draconian prison wasn't enough!* I was still grieving for my darling Cindy, and now I had this hassle to go though.

It was a shame Twiki and Theo weren't with us on Dracos.  Then again, would you want to take *them* to Dracos?  At least they could have protested for my innocence.  Silage, I knew, was not so innocent.  He was planning to remain there indefinitely.  He was planning to find a wife or wives for marriage, until I barged in, pretending to be him. He was giving the Emperor information of all sorts. I felt embarrassed about the whole debacle; maybe Cindy and I should have stayed behind and enjoyed ourselves privately.  *Leave my brother out of this.*

The prison was just as spartan as the one on Dracos.  I still had Cindy then, so the Draconian prison was more palatable.  This one just had me and Silage, and no one else.  We were put in solitary, but at least we were still together.  It would be a waste of a cell to put just one person in each.  I gave Silage a few harsh looks.  It was bad enough Dad's idea of Silage going to Dracos for his advanced education was a 'good' one.  It became worse because it led to my wife's death and our current incarceration.

'Don't worry brother,' Silage tried to soothe me, 'We'll get out of this one.  We are innocent after all.'

'I am innocent, not you,' I ranted, 'None of your dozy spells will get us out of this.'

He went into a corner, and began to chant.  I tut-tutted to myself about it and sat down, with my hands covering my face.  The minutes-long silence made you hear a pin drop.  I didn't want to disturb him.  *Maybe we could get out of here.*  I tried to remember that Bible; I was certain that there were people in *those* days who went through terrible times, prison and other firelocks of despair, and they came through all right.  *Well, most of the time.*

Most of the time those ancient beings, who put their trust in an imaginary presence, usually got hit first. That imaginary presence was always being challenged. I reckoned that was why Julian gave the book to me, and tried to increase my faith in the same, called God. Truthfully, I didn't care at the time, and I still didn't. My brother did, though, and he seemed strong enough to take it.

# CHAPTER IV

Hours later, we were taken into another room full of brightly coloured discs of Christmas lights that had flourished. They bleeped and buzzed, flickering embers of light concurring with the dockets ahead. The whole Computer Council had set this trial up; convincing *them* won't be easy.

Theo was there, placed on our side of the podium. 'Hello Elias, it had been some time since we last spoke. Congratulations on your stargate discovery.'

'Well, look where it got us,' I murmured back.

'I heard about your wife Cindy,' the unit commiserated in his own fashion, 'And I am terribly sorry about that. I will be counsel to you and Silas.'

'Great,' I smirked.

We were hushed up by a robot box council member, as Pemur had placed Dr Ruckus in his station as the opposing faction. He was not someone to turn to for sympathy; he was a circuit, full of mathematically stubborn independence, and a prickly personality for a sentient life form. I wondered who, or what, had a tree up his ass to construct such a creature. Ruckus took the floor with a commanding presence scarier than a sea captain of old.

He began the ordeal. 'The two parties Elias Huer and Silas Huer are hereby charged with collusion with a foreign entity. Have you anything to say before I continue?'

Silage and I looked at one another, then at Theo. Theo calmly interpreted our meanings. 'No, we don't. Please resume your findings.'

'Thank you,' Ruckus flashed his wits about him. 'Elias Huer and his wife, Cindihan Huer had discovered a stargate. By the way, where is Mrs Huer?'

'Deceased, sir,' Theo said.

'Okay, we will get to that later.  To surmise, Elias and Cindihan were on their way back after discovering the stargate, when their ship's battery needed to recharge.  Is that correct?'

'Yes,' Theo added.

'To recharge the battery, they had to land somewhere.  They chose to land on the Saturn moon of Dracos.'

Theo spoke. 'That is correct; the ship's records state so.  While waiting for the ship to complete its cycle, they went to visit Silas Huer, who had been living there for some time.'

'Fine.  I want to call Silas Huer to the stand.'

Silage got up, went to the surround box, and swore to tell the truth on a Bible. I found it funny how the Council saw fit to make us swear by primitive writings that humans valued most of all.  We could have sworn by something a little more recent with the same beliefs.

Ruckus addressed him. 'You are Silas Huer, son of Elias Huer, Sr.'

'I am,' Silage responded.

'You are the twin brother of one Elias Huer, Jr.'

'I am.'

'Are you close to him?'

'Only recently we've made a bond together.  Beforehand, no.  We were not close at all.'

Ruckus knew this type of rivalry. 'Adversarial?'

'Yes.'

'What was the purpose of your duration on Dracos?'

'I attended the Academy and lived there for awhile.'

'Did you intend on returning to New Chicago?'

'No.'

'Why?'

'I liked Dracos and found it culturally fascinating.'

'How so?'

Silage heaved a sigh, slightly impatiently saying, 'I liked learning about history and culture of other peoples, and how they coped after the Big Blast.'

'So you were keen to explore this new territory for yourself?'

'Yes.'

'What were you doing on Dracos after your education?'

'Small jobs in the Emperor Hansfor's service.'

'Doing what?'

'Serving his needs.'

'What needs?'

'Information.'

The other computer's lights cackled within their stout cases, already forming a verdict.  Of course, they were willing to listen on, just to see if they were correct in their formations.  They did not want to come across as a hung jury.

Ruckus went on.  'What were you to do with any information you gained to serve this Emperor?'

'To give it to him, I suppose,' Silage answered.

'What did the Emperor ask of you with respect to Elias Huer?'

'To find out the purpose of his visit.'

Ruckus ploughed on to the heart of the matter. 'Were you aware of Elias and Cindihan's discovery of the stargate?'

'Not at first, no.'

'How did you find out about it?'

Silage hesitated a little.  Ruckus was not having any of it.

'Silas Huer, how did you find out about the stargate?'

My brother squirmed a bit more before uttering, 'By magic, sir.'

The Computer Council lit up wildly.  'Magic,' they cried out.

Ruckus was astounded.  'You attained information from your brother using magic?'

'I did,' came Silage's answer.

'Well, I will dare not ask what you magically did to conjure up this information.  Once you attained the information, what did you do?'

'I was to go to Emperor Hansfor and tell him directly.'

'And did you?'

'No. I did not.'

'What prevented you from seeing the Emperor?'

'My brother Elias, with his wife Cindy, put me to sleep, using my spell-book.  I do not know what happened next.'

'Thank you, Silas Huer.  Dr Theopolis, do you have any questions for this defendant?'

'Yes I do,' said our friendly boxed unit, which I hoped would get us out of this chaos.

'Proceed,' came the answer from the humdrum Ruckus.

Theo kept to his usual placid self. 'Silas Huer, you stated that you learned of the stargate through magic, is that correct?'

'Yes,' he said.

'Might I enquire how you did it?'

'I had a book on spells that was with me through my childhood days. I used a mind swap spell to gain entrance into my brother's mind to find out his whereabouts and why he came to Dracos.'

'I thought your brother had to land on Dracos to recharge the ship,' Theo sneered.

'That is what Elias and Cindihan told me.  They also thought it would be a good idea to visit me, too.  I figured there were other possibilit- ies, so I waited for an opportunity to see what transpired.'

'I see.  You were close to the Draconian Emperor?'

'Close enough to tell him your visions.'

The onlookers laughed and tittered for a bit, when Ruckus demanded quiet.

Theo continued, trying to entertain the subject. 'I have no visions to tell anyone.  We have no visions.  And what were your visions?'

'I saw my brother and his wife keeping something from me.  I do not know why.  I just did, and I had to investigate.'

'For imperial reasons?'

'Yes.' Silage began to squirm a bit.

'Do sit still, Mr Huer,' Theo complained, 'You are spoiling *my* circuits of vision.'

The room fell ablaze with more laughter, and the Computer Council wondered if it was all worth it, with us being made out to look like fools, thanks to Silage!

Ruckus screamed, 'Silence!'

Theo asked, 'How did you perform the mind-swap spell you previously referred to?'

'I chanted words that were in the book, but I cannot remember them now. I then was able to see through into his mentality and realised he was hiding something: the knowledge of the stargate. He then got into my mind, putting me to sleep, and paraded around as if he were me, even wearing my clothes. Thus, the spell went both ways; because the discovery of the stargate was foremost in his mind at that time, it was easy to read it.'

'Can you read minds on your own or with the help of resources, such as a spell book?'

'I would need the book.'

Theo's unit-pack was becoming critically overstressed with this information, so crazy as it was. 'And where is the book now?'

'I left it behind on Dracos, because Elias and I were hurried away to our ship to return here. We did not have time to pack our belongings, and we also had Cindihan to deal with. I do not know what became of the book.'

The lone drone unit sighed, 'No further questions, please. I need to recalibrate my chambers.'

'You may go,' Ruckus dismissed Silage.

The human onlookers still laughed at the earlier comments and the computer's lights whizzed with processing in reddish tones, as if they were blushing with confused agitation. Here they were, trying a case against us, and with a flick of unadulterated words, they lay bare as exposed wires of light.

Within this process, one of the computers went slightly faulty. It puttered, sputtered, and spewed up a minor firework show. A recess had to be passed for the morning. Silage and I were led out by Pemur, who took us under his wing for the rest of the day.

'What you experienced is truly phenomenal in its own right,' Pemur said, 'However, I won't be condescending to either of you, so would you like to go out for something to eat?'

It was a hearty wish on my part; Silage agreed. 'Sure,' he said.

'Good, I know somewhere that's good and has privacy so we can discuss your case. I'll bring Twiki and Theo so we can go over it together.'

'Thanks,' Silage added.

Soon, the pair-in-one unit came by to see us. Theo's recalibration was taking place, as he engaged in conversation with Silage.

'You were good on the stand today, Silas,' Theo complimented, 'But I had to ask if there was any further testimony on your part which they could scrutinise. I'm sorry about that. I had to ask you those questions to elaborate your testimony about the so-called magic and spells you used to gain information for the Draconians.'

Silage smiled at the small box of lights and realised they were more than just a flash in the moment. They could make or break his life. *Mine, too.* They sizzled in front of him, dashing about, faster than any of his silly mythological figures could muster. Silage stayed silent and was weary from his time in the surround box and nearly collapsed, fearing he'd be an equivalent of a 25th century heretic. Being part of a flame at the stake would be most welcome in such tedious circumstances.

Pemur held him steady and gave him a drink.

'Your time will come too, Elias,' he said to me.

I gulped and feared what would come from a box of Christmas lights who meant business. My heart gave in to pain, as I grimaced at my brother, who understood.

He came to me and gave me a hug. 'I forgive you for disliking my actions, Brother Elias.'

I was surprised he used that epithet in this awkward circumstance. I didn't care anymore, as he was all I had as family. Nothing could surpass that.

When this was all over, we both could get married and attend each others weddings, and our children will be caught up in cousinry. I mused upon this, but I had a feeling it would never become attainable. Silage had a way of the tragic about him, believing in things that were not really part of our reality. *Maybe someone else's, but not ours*. I myself yielded toward science, with a small trip over the spiritual when needed. I was proud of that, somewhat. At this time though, I felt I really needed it.

# CHAPTER V

It was time for me to be heard, as I was called to the stand. Silage wished me well and it was my turn to be interrogated by the box of non-stop flaming lights. Like a cow brain in a western, smothered in dust, I approached the stand. Dr Ruckus had thrown the usual fare at me, with the Bible present and swearing-in ceremony.

He asked me, 'You are Elias Huer, Jr.?'

'I am.'

'You have a twin brother, Silas Huer?'

'Yes I do.'

'What were you doing when your brother Silas went off to Dracos for educational purposes?'

I sighed, 'My father sent me to Anarchia. He thought it would be good for me to get away from the comforts of New Chicago.'

Ruckus was intrigued by hearing about the outer areas. 'What was it like there?'

'Desolate, sir.'

'Did you meet anyone in particular?'

'My late wife Cindihan Huer.'

I began to cry a bit, showing more defencelessness than I had ever portrayed.

Ruckus wasn't concerned though.  'Calm yourself Mr Huer!'

The computers flashed their lights about in conversation.

Ruckus went on. 'How long had you been with her in marriage?'

'A few years now.'

'Did she accompany you on that exploration in space, when you dis-covered the stargate?'

'Yes she did.'

'I surmise she was with you when you were on Dracos.'

'That is correct.'

'What was your purpose on Dracos?'

*That question bugged me, as that was what the Draconians were asking about as well!*

I answered, 'To recharge my ship.'

'Was there another reason?'

'To visit my brother.'

'Ah, so you wanted to spend time with someone who you barely got along with.'

'I thought it was the right thing to do.'

Ruckus was adamant to get to the bottom of it all. 'Did you have any intention to reveal your travels to the Draconian Emperor?'

Now, it was me who was adamant. 'No I did not.'

'How did you prevent the information from getting to the Draconian Emperor?'

'When my brother did the mind-swap spell on me, I used his magic book to put him to sleep, so I could see the Emperor myself.'

'Did you do this on your own or with your wife?'

'My wife helped me, but I did the deed.'

'All this magic sounds stupid to us computers.  What was the point of it?'

'My brother Silas was keen on the topic since childhood and he used it to get into my mind, hence the mind-swap, and find out what our purpose on Dracos was.'

'So he suspected another reason for your visit?'

'Yes, and so did the Draconians.'

'So out of your human desperation and wish to conceal information about your discovery, you put him to sleep with a spell.'

'That is correct.'

'So I trust you and Mrs Huer went to see the Emperor in Silas's stead.'

'No.  I told my wife to look for our ship, so we could leave.'

'Did she find it?'

'Yes, but she was caught by the Draconians and incarcerated as a prisoner.'

'What did you say to the Emperor when you did see him as Silas Huer?'

'I told him there was a hole in space, an old star that died out many years ago.'

'Did the Emperor believe you?'

'Yes.'

'Then what happened?'

'I was allowed to find a wife for myself, as Silas would have.'

'So your so-called spell trick worked.'

'Yes.'

'So you did not tell the Emperor about the stargate.'

'No, I did not, and did not want to.'

'So by putting your brother to sleep as you say, you were able to go in his stead, give this Emperor a crafty story, as it were, in order to save yourself?'

'Yes.  I did it for the Directorate because I knew if the Draconians were aware of a stargate in the outer systems, they would use it to conquer planets beyond it.'

'What made you think that?'

'Their overall societal attitudes and demeanour, sir.'

'What happened to your wife after she was captured by the Draconians?'

'A Draconian shot her, because we kept silent about the stargate. A form of punishment, as it were. Before then, we had another meeting with the Emperor, and Silas was about to reveal our mission when he choked up. At that point, my wife was shot.  As we proved useless to the Draconians, and the Emperor's granddaughter was just born recently, they let us go at that point, and told us never to return again.'

'So there was no mention of the stargate?'

'No, there was no mention of the stargate.'

Ruckus let out a heavy sigh, reflecting the nonsense that he heard, and asked his colleague, 'Dr Theopolis, do you have any questions for the defendant, Elias Huer?'

The circular unit twiddled and twaddled a few moments before responding.  'Yes, I do.'

The superior of the two units went on. 'Please proceed.'

With a high powered glare and thoughtful resolution, Theo began to embroil me in a way that would make an ancient television jealous. 'Mr Huer, could you please relate what you understand to be the events in sequence?'

'I have already told you what happened and in what order it happened,' I insisted.

'Could you please explain what you mean by mind swap?'

'Why don't you ask Silas that? He's the genius behind everything,' I yelled back emotionally.

'I had done so already.  Now, I am asking you, rather calmly, I might add, so please cooperate,' Theo replied coolly.

My insides felt like a twisted version of an old symbol with two colours casing in on one another.  I tried to explain this the best I could. 'Silas tried to get the information out of me by trickery of the mind. The spell he used was from a book he had and read since childhood; it was supposed to swap his mind into mine, and vice versa.'

'So you are not truly understanding what is meant by spells or magic, as used by your brother Silas?'

'No.  I am firmly into science and reality. I only know the nonsense my brother believes in as spells or magic, because that is what they were called by him,' I answered.

Theo' s inquisitiveness disturbed me.  His lights continued to twiddle and swill before my eyes.

'At any point in the events on Dracos, did you have any objective to mention to the Emperor about the stargate?'

And I continued my rant. 'Not at all!  As I have already said that I understood the risk for other planets, should the Draconians find out about the stargate. I considered all the possibilities, such as the conquests, and the embattled people whom they would enslave. That is why I kept silent on Dracos. It is not my fault my brother found the answer in my head.'

The drone humoured me.  'Clearly it is not.'

'But I made certain that he would choke on the word 'stargate' the moment it was mentioned aloud,' I smiled crudely.

Theo was already frazzled by the notion, and dismissed me.  'Thank you, Elias Huer.  You may go.  We shall adjourn until tomorrow morning when we reach our verdict.'

The computers all buzzed about to one another, with Ruckus joining in their light-show.  Silage and I went back to the prison.  We sat in the boring room with crap decor staring outward toward one another. I felt sorry about the mess we landed in, and Silage was now thinking Anarchia sounded more interesting than Dracos.  It was better out there, and I think he would have loved the primitiveness of that lot of people.  Then again, he would have gone after Cindy a lot sooner, probably would have taken her for his own.  I didn't want to dwell on that, considering she was now gone and he became a close ally to me.

Losing my own family would have been worse than just losing a wife. Right now, all I cared about was getting the Directorate off our backs about this.

I knew in my own way, the stargate was classified information, but this hounding was becoming uncharacteristically persecutory. Nothing made sense and I wanted Cindy. Without her, I was nothing; a mere shadow of my father. Silage was unlike Dad in every way, and continued to be so.

I started to cry about Cindy again, as the deflated atmosphere of this place wore me down.

'Elias, it is no good to be tearful,' Silage cradled me, 'I know how much she meant to you and it is difficult to accept she's gone, but she is not gone from your heart.'

I sniffed and blurted out, 'All your fine witchery couldn't get her back, could it?'

'I'm so sorry.'

'I had to get past your wall of wives, just to survive in that Palace!'

'I guess that stun had no stunning effects,' Silage said.

'Yeah,' I huffed.

At this point, I had no feelings, but the coldness of space to comfort me. Silage went to the window and stared at the buildings there and those with huge frames about to be built. He heaved a heavy sigh and was greatly upset his actions came to this.

'I'm going to bed,' he walked toward the bunk and took the lower half.

'Fine.'

He climbed in, silently nodding off without a wink.  I never felt so alone in my life.  Even Twiki would have made a better companion, and with Theo attached to him, the pair would have lit up another universe for me.  I began to nod off in my chair, when a buzzer sounded.  It didn't matter who it was.  A visitor was a visitor, and a jailer was a jailer.

'Yeah,' I called out, 'Come in.'

'Hiya, Elias,' a familiar sassy voice spoke.

I got up. 'Twiki?'

'Yep boss, it's me.'

Theo chimed in, 'It is good to see you Elias, but it is not looking good for either of you.'

'The Computer Council is still in session?'

'Yes.  They are still arguing about the verdict.  The majority of them want to see you hang, along with your brother, because you had a nerve to visit another planet when you housed sensitive information.'

'I had no wish to tell the Draconians. I told you; I came to that conclusion myself. You never told me to hush-up about it.'

Theo's lights flashed wildly at me.  'No we did not, but then again, you did not plan to visit the foreign moon, did you?'

'We only went to Dracos to recharge.  Meg could tell you that.  While the ship recharged, Cindy and I decided to see our brother.  That was it.'

'I know that, I conferred with the ship.  The Council knows too, but they believe there was motive in your journey and with the information you gave us, we will decide what is best for you.'

I shouted in desperation, 'I know what is best for me.  Get me out of here and into the lab!'

'Brother Elias, please let me sleep,' Silage complained, 'You just woke me up.'

I regretted my action. 'Sorry.'

'You could use some sleep, Elias Huer,' Theo suggested, 'I will leave you and return in the morning.'

The pair walked out and we were left to ourselves to sleep.  I tried my damnedest to fall into dreams, but I knew they'd become nightmares.  I was afraid of what would come of us; Silage nor I, wished to think upon it.  Silage was already back in his dozy conical of rest; I had a much more difficult time of it.  I guessed the morning should bring about a fair result.

# CHAPTER VI

The sun streamed in with an inviting warmth that made you want to face the day, even if it wasn't worth facing. I opened my eyes to find Silage wading through the air, facing another window, with his chanting. The trial felt long, consisting of the Computer Council, Silage and me. Though it was only a couple of days, with us just being questioned, it felt like centuries. I had to accept that Cindy was dead, and that Draconian fellow, Buckwolf, who came aboard our ship, was already sent back to the Saturn moon, *so I was told*. I had a feeling, though, he might have been killed.

Not that our society was better than that of the Draconians, but there were exceptions. The information I held was too much for the Council, and for all I know, they might have ordered a quiet execution for Buckwolf. Dracos would never see him again. The Computer Council's take on justice did not allow for human frailties. Unless they were convinced heavily with sound argument that there *were* frailties in the first place, the Council needed to make allowances for them.

A guard came by to wake us up and serve breakfast. At least there were some niceties around here. Silage and I ate, when Pemur, Twiki and Theo arrived.

'Good morning,' Pemur greeted us.

'Hi,' Silage nodded.

I simply waved, having a mouthful of rations at the time.

'They're ready to pass the verdict,' Pemur said.

'Thank you,' I garbled, 'But can we finish eating first?'

'Of course. I'll wait outside.  Tell the guard when you're ready.'

Twiki waved to us and beaded away with Theo.  It seemed that Theo already knew what action the Council decided on.  I figured that was why he was so quiet; Twiki's usually the noisy one anyway.  I admired their dependability and the feeling that they were always watching you, kind of like a god of the old days.  I laughed to myself, thinking if Twiki and Theo went back in time, to Silage's favourite epochs, they would be considered gods themselves. I supposed the beading away would freak people out, though.

About a half hour later, we were ready to meet our judgment.  We were taken back to the room full of those sentient lights covered in hard boxes.  I'd almost like to think this was a joke, if the nature of our time on Dracos hadn't become so serious.  The Computer Council posted their verdict, as our tiresome mess was beyond their circuits.  At least the questioning was succinct; straight and to the point.  I hated to imagine if this trial of ours would have been conducted by humans; it would have dragged on for months.  Computers were more literal in their findings, and how they got to them worked wonders on the calendar.  They didn't care about us as such; all they cared about was running a functional society where *they* were the norm.

Ruckus was wheeled forward and announced his verdict.  'Silas Huer, as you demonstrated intentions to remain on Dracos, possibly giving up your citizenship on Earth, and in collusion with the Draconians to obtain information that would further their progress into other galaxies, I sentence you to execution.'

A gasp from the humans present was overheard.  Pemur and Silage looked double-shocked at one another, and I remained silent, but hopeful.

Ruckus didn't give two lights about *anyone's* reactions and read on. 'Elias Huer, Jr, your attempted discretion of discovering the stargate was admirable, since no one told you to keep it from the Draconians.'

After a tense pause, the unit continued.  'In light of this, and due to your widowed status, you will be doing hard labour for the next ten years; from which you may return to the Directorate and serve in the capacity your father excelled at.  Good day.'

The flashy lights then dimmed, as the computer was wheeled away to return to his chambers.  The other computers stood down and sat there aloof like a still, silent drummer. I was overcome with further grief, and wanted to shriek blue murder at those lights.  Another fa-milial loss was too much, even if I didn't like Silage. *He was still my brother.* Nothing could stop my wild permeations of protest toward the Council.

'I cannot believe this.  He is sentenced to die,' I yelled out. 'Aaauugghh!'

Pemur saw my enraged face and said, 'Well, what did you expect from boxes of cavorting Christmas lights?'

He embraced me firmly, as I struggled to remain calm in all this mad-ness.  Silage was to be taken away like a so-called traitor and 'shot at dawn', or something of the sort.  He didn't move an inch, and showed no passion.  In fact, he took it as it came to him, and he accepted the fate he was given.  We were let out and put into different cells this time.  I protested greatly and hotly, as Silage was put away with the damned.  No advancement of being was ensued and we were separ-ated for good. It would be the final time I saw him alive.

Pemur followed me into the cell.  'You okay, Elias?'

I gave him a scowl and shook my head. 'Duh, what do you think?'

He stared thoughtfully at me. 'I think you are a devastated young man.'

'I'm not that young, but I am clearly devastated,' I stated gruffly.

'I'll try to get leniency for you, so you needn't spend ten years of your life on that farm. Hang in there, I'll figure something out.'

'What about Silas?'

'What about him?  You don't even like him, ' Pemur stated.

'He's all I got.  Aren't you going to help him?'

Pemur gave me a glimmer of hope.  *Some hope.* 'I'll try.  His use of the archaic crafts may be used against him, as we don't believe in that ancient claptrap.  You know what the Council's like.'

*Yeah, I sure do.  Cold, calculating and BORING!*

'Led by that Ruckus fellow,' I pouted, this time in Cindy's honour.

'Don't worry about Ruckus.  He's getting on, you know,' Pemur explained, 'One of our earlier models.  I do admit he was a little harsh with you two.'

I exclaimed, 'A little harsh?'

'I know, I know,' he reassured me, 'I must say that Silas had put our work in jeopardy, in trying to find out about the stargate.'

'I took it upon myself not to disclose the information.'

'That will be taken into consideration, as well as your wife's death, points already mentioned at the trial.  Ruckus made a minor attempt at 'feeling' for you, and had deliberated intensely about it. That's what took so long, and why you are being sent to a work camp and not the electric chair.'

He put his hand on my shoulder and bade farewell to me.  He walked away and left me to my own devices, except I didn't have any.  There was a whole load of hope and a whole none of Cindy.  I began to weep again over her and this time, I couldn't contain myself.  Her funeral came and went, but the memory of such a strong woman continued to linger in my mind, along with all the crazy adventures and love we both shared together.  It wasn't the same without her, and deep in my heart, something was changing. *It wasn't one of Silage's trickster spells, oh no.*  It was something else, something more to be discovered, at a later date.

# CHAPTER VII

It was my own will that made me think of what my future would be like.  I thought about Dad, his scientific work, and how everyone told me I would be like him, even Dr Ruckus.  *Maybe I could do it.*  At least, it would keep me in the Directorate's control; but I disliked the notion, thinking any form of control was nothing more than draconian.  Still, I'd make myself into a useful entity, indulging in my private experiments, perhaps making more fulfilling discoveries, apart from the stargate.  I kept thinking about the Januard entity, now knowing it was a ship, and thought to explore it more fully.  I remember Cindy and I seeing this ship, just floating out in space like an antique frozen morsel of *something*.  It could be something I could ask Pemur about and delve into on another level.

To which his reply came to me during another visit, 'We ain't spending money to excavate an old Earth ship!'

*So much for personal ingenuity.*

'Oh, why not?'  I looked at him.

'Your integrity is in question, you know,' he explained, 'We don't have the time nor resources for you or someone else to go on another crazy expedition.'

'But you let Cindy and I go out before,' I yelped.

'Yes, however, you entangled yourself with the Draconians.'

'I was trying to save my brother from himself.'

'You stated that you had to recharge the ship.'

'That too.'

Pemur's patience with me got the better of him.  'What you need is to return to the Directorate under my tutelage and study.'

I pondered this and decided it would be a good idea, once the punishment I would undergo was dealt out.

'You could use your father's old office as well, if you want,' he said.

'Will you get me off the ten year duration; make it shorter or something,' I pleaded.

'I will see what I can do,' he replied, 'But convincing the Council, especially Dr Ruckus, will be quite a challenge.'

'Buck off,' I puffed steam at him, 'You must.  You know I would never betray the Directorate, or the Earth for that matter!'

'Okay, okay,' Pemur resigned to his task.  'But first, we get you to that work farm, so you can settle down and stay out of the way, while I try to help you.  Your temperament isn't helping matters, you know.'

I nodded, 'I do know, and I am sorry for cursing you out.'

'I've been called worse,' he smiled. 'I will be in touch.'

He walked out of my cell, which got relocked upon his exit.  I sat down and kept away from everything and everybody for the time being.  A meal was brought in.  Short and sweet, but bland and bitter to the taste.  I couldn't eat, but I wasn't in shape to fight anymore.  I was in a sour state of being and life was sharply intense for me.

Pemur would go to the Computer Council and argue for my case, with regards to lessening my sentence.  Later on, when he met up with the string of lit boxes, he presented his postulations to them. The Council simply looked upon him as a foolish mortal, trying to come up with excuses for his own responsibilities, *namely me*.  He also attempted to have a word regarding Silage.

The Council, with Ruckus in the lead, still did not back down.

'No,' Dr Ruckus proclaimed, 'Silas Huer is to be executed and Elias sent away for his own good. We are not running a sideshow here.'

Pemur was beside himself. 'How could you treat such prominent people in that manner?'

'When they do not act in a manner befitting their place in our society,' came the lit-up answer. 'It was built from the bottom up and we will not allow you humans to run around rampant here.'

'But they did not reveal the stargate to the Draconians,' Pemur yelled.

'That is true,' Theo then chimed in, 'But wouldn't you think the Huers' actions on Dracos constitute a form of collusion?'

Pemur started to split hairs, but these computers didn't have hair.  'Alright, I admit they used rather unorthodox methods to keep the information to themselves, and Silas had used his so-called powers to get into Elias's mind, but again, the stargate was never mentioned to the Draconians.'

Theo presumed with him.  It was as arduous as climbing a mountain that no longer exists.  Pemur was already mentally exhausted.

The unit chimed back, 'Don't you think it is rather crass of one to get into someone else's mind to obtain private information?  What if Silas Huer had told them about it, then what?'

'Then we'd be in trouble.  But he didn't.  Elias took over, to work for our benefit.  Despite us not telling him his discovery was classified, he knew better.  He used initiative, completely on his own, in order to save our cause, possibly saving the universe.'

'And his wife was killed for it,' Ruckus brightly blurted out.

Pemur rubbed his forehead, after a spent penny of silence murmured through the room.  'So this is your final judgment, huh?  No reprieve?  No time off for good behaviour and so forth?'

Ruckus was firm about it and stood his ground.  'Rules are rules.  The Huers were dealing with a foreign race, and Elias carried secret information.  He put himself and his wife in danger by going to Dracos for a family visit, despite his statement about recharging the ship.'

Pemur was aghast.  'You still don't believe that, do you?  The computers on *The Ancient Crab* indicated a recharge of the system.'

'Yes, but computers do not reveal ulterior motives,' Theo passively stated.

The human gave up in the end.  'So I have no choice, then.  You will throw away a person's life for the sake of your sanities, yeah?'

The unanimous Council emitted a sound together, that sounded like something you did that was rather rude.  Sometimes, computers could be 'human', but only when they show utter disgust.

'We will reassess Elias Huer's judgment, but we will not budge for Silas,' Ruckus declared, 'At least, Elias showed a bit of discretion. Silas had no scruples about him during this whole debacle. He showed intention to inform the Draconians, and that is why he must be punished. Any leakage of what we discover, could mean catastrophe for our world.'

Pemur started to walk out on them, then hesitated. 'Please, will you reconsider the circumstances regarding Silas? Surely there is a tremor or two in your circuitry for mercy.'

The computers fluctuated and gave a bright display, but it wasn't a light-show as such. The endless flickering gave hope to Pemur, as he watched them debate, yet again.

'There are no tremors in our circuitry to rock old California. Silas Huer has been deemed a traitor by us,' Ruckus reprimanded him, 'You humans are too sentimental in your tactics. No wonder you went through hundreds of years of miscarried legal cases. Sheesh!'

With deep regret and hatred for those apathetic units, Pemur announced. 'I'll go tell them.'

'You do that,' Ruckus taunted after him. 'You do that.'

He left the room, with a weighty burden in his heart. A peal of laughter would have been appropriate after this, but these computers, having no emotion of any kind, would just state *their* facts and leave you out in the cold. They certainly did that to Pemur. As a friend to us Huer brothers, he was aghast that the Council found him 'sentimental', demonstrating that human justice was imperfect.

Even in the sleek time of the 25$^{th}$ century, there was no need for absolute perfection. Pemur knew their programming, especially that of Dr Ruckus, was a little too discordant. The infinite feeling that he had about the opposing unit reverberated in his mind; that is, to shut him down. The silicone chips, housed in that circular base of his, had given this unit a bleak perspective on life. Everything had to be computer-perfect.

Yet, he knew programs could be changed, but attitudes in life and conduct, now that was another matter altogether. It was another thing to contemplate; maybe making them a little more human-friendly. Then Pemur remembered one vital aspect. *These computers programmed themselves*. Well, in that case, there was no hope for humanity in this distant whirl of technology. It was very easy to see how the creation could rebel against the creator.

# CHAPTER VIII

Dracos, meanwhile, underwent a change in leadership. The old Emperor Hansfor had passed away, leaving his son Draco to take the reins of the young Empire. The middle-aged son had been busy recently with preparations of the change, as well as keeping all of his wives occupied. There were so many of them, he forgot to count them all; Ardala was not his only child, but she was the first. As she was growing into a stirring Draconian princess, there were many other female children, born and bred to take her place, should she prove otherwise. Ardala knew the importance of her role in life, and her realm; she constantly was fighting off the fury of the multitude of sisters she had to endure, as she found them to be 'getting in the way of things'.

The Saturn moon that was home to the Draconians, proved too diminutive to the Empire-bound people. They were heavily into conquering new worlds, while taking over established worlds. Yet, the current star system was limited, and the other moons in the vicinity were unfeasible. So they took it upon themselves toward betterment and reached out into mortal space. Remembering the Huers visit to their pivotal orbit, they tried to figure out the farthest place where they could go, in order for them to go back and land on their moon. Despite not knowing the exact location, the Draconians took exploration pods outward bound and had a good look beyond the solar system. Their intuition paid off, and the four-star anomaly appeared into view and activated upon entry.

The Draconian pilots were as meaty as fire and tough as shit. They were excited at this new fissure in the galaxy, and plotted on to see what lay beyond these stars. They narrowly missed the Januard entity, never-minding it as it passed. There were new worlds out there, and the Draconians were hungry with delight in *their* discovery.

The people of Dracos could look forward to more elbow room these new planets had to offer.  There was certainly plenty to choose from, among all the planets they came across in these latter quadrants.

One of the pilots reported to Silver Kane, who was in communications. 'I think we've found a new pasture to graze in.  There is much exploring to do.  There are hundreds of planets out here.  We could live on one, sir.'

'Good work,' Kane replied, thinking this was what the Huers were keeping from them. 'Yes, we will live on one, maybe many, once we know what or who we are dealing with.  Come back to base.'

'Roger that and over.'

The ship veered back to the stargate, with its starry eyed presence and the familiarity of the outer solar system appeared.  Pluto, Neptune, Uranus.  There was definitely worth something to spread around the galaxy with, taking in one planet at a time.  Dracos could trade with them, or enslave them. It was just too good to ask for, and the afterthought went toward Elias Huer, because he had flown through this entity before.  Silver Kane and his brother, Antssarah Kane had desperately wanted to please the Emperor and with Silas around, they felt they could do that.

With Elias and his wife's visit, they thought they could find out where they've been.  Silas would have seen to that, but it didn't work out that way, and the Draconians had to find it out for themselves. *Maybe Elias and Cindy did the Draconians a favour.*  As the Draconians discovered the stargate on their own, without the Huers' assistance, more glory be unto them.  It was an achievement to be proud of and something to take advantage of.

They certainly would take advantage of it, maybe settling upon a new planet, so their society could grow beyond the Saturn moon.

One day, Emperor Draco decided he had enough of the small moon and hauled his ship toward the stargate.  His little world was getting smaller, and it did not allow for population growth after a time. It was time to declutter, and find more space for his people. So, he had his whole planet relocated beyond the stargate, settling on another world and calling it after himself, Draco.  He was keen to own these new worlds, and made his armies ready for their delicious conquests in space.  *If a small moon left no opposition, what were these planets and moons like?  We could take over the entire galaxy.*  The thought pressed in the new Emperor's mind, and he was quite pleased with it.

He banded his armies together, and one by one, all the planets became his own; conquered and with some fight, but mostly untouched until now.  The yelping daughters, with Ardala in the forefront, made for grand family moments, as one by one Draconian might proved too much for the smaller entities of planets and moons.  Even the asteroids yielded to Draconian mastery of the universe.  Eventually, the star system beyond the stargate succumbed to Draconian rule. The vanquished peoples of those planets didn't mind, because they felt the Draconians knew better. Though some of them tried to oppose the rulers, most of the people decided it wasn't worth it.  Draco finally had his time and kept his ruling a rather peaceful one.

Once Ardala came of age, she got her own ship, the *Draconia*, manned by troops helmeted like the Samurai of old. That little girl was a whirlwind of promise.  Silver Kane aspired to get into the upper echelons of government and he felt serving alongside the Princess would get him there.

It was undetermined who was really in charge, as Kane would chastise the Princess if she stepped out of line.  Yet, being a Princess gave Ardala more power and leeway over him. She was given a bodyguard, Tigerman, who watched over her like a hawk. Given all these advantages in life, Ardala had the upper hand.  It would be compelling to see where she takes them.

# CHAPTER IX

I awaited my orders to go to the temporary accommodation on this work farm, as I came to terms with Cindy's death, Silage's fate, and my destiny, somewhere within the Directorate. Pemur promised me a position in the science branch where he was, so that one day, I may take over and run it myself. First, I needed to mend.

The men in light blue full-dress outfits led me away to Nuconnalow, for people in need of confinement, love and support. It wasn't a funny farm, nor the workhouse that I thought it would be. Pemur saw to that. It was mutually comfortable surroundings, where those within society who cracked could come here to unwind, with a price. They had to help out with things, anything. It wasn't a prison, so that was good, but you couldn't escape either. At least Pemur got my sentence down to about a year from the original ten. The Computer Council obviously deemed my version of events to be factual, but the unusualness of it baffled them. They still refused to budge regarding Silage. He was sentenced and doomed to die. That was unwavering; he intended to remain on Dracos, and in order to secure information, he used his silly powers for ill-gain.

I was insulted that I had to be put here, without the familiarity of my own surroundings. It was okay, somewhat; institutionalised, definitely. It didn't feel like an institution, though. Yet, with all this in mind, I began to unravel at the seams, and it didn't look good for me. It was apparent in my early weeks there, I started to crack wide open without hesitation. People who witnessed me reported some violent tendencies on my part. This wasn't surprising, given the mental state I was in. Unfortunately, it wasn't one of the states of the union.

I still fancied stargazing and loved looking up at the sky. Newly made Runnabug Scout-fighters flew by, with their emissions mixing within the clouds, creating their own stamp overhead.

I reflected on the name of Nuconnalow, which reminded me of the old Irish town of Oconnalow, the place where real people told a good story and drank a mean pint.  They still did this, though in the more sanitised conditions of the 25th century.

Overall, I was happy here, but the confinement became pressing and unnecessary.  I needed to get out of these surroundings and find my way toward the science of my father.  Those mean pints of the past could have done wonders here.  The foremen wouldn't let you, though. If they did, they'd probably want some too, and you didn't want to share!

A radio station played music to sooth us.  A song played in the background called *The Day New 'Cago Rose (From the Ashes)*.  I listened to it, from its beginning, describing the Big Blast, to the slick-sheen, shiny-clean wonder of our nowadays. New Chicago had risen from whatever ashes there were, proverbial or otherwise.  The tail end of the song had an odd prophesy about it:

*There was once a man from space*
*Who crash landed on the human race.*
*It has been 500 years,*
*And despite all the tears,*
*You should have seen the look on his face.*

I thought about that Januard ship and wondered if there was a connection.  At the time, I didn't think anyone would be on that derelict vehicle, and they forbade me from exploring it.

Another song had played odd melody and lyrics to boot, which reminded me of Cindy, but someone of long ago; maybe an ancestor. One part of it went something like this:

Meanwhile, I was assigned to gardening duties to allow me to work and enjoy the fresh air. They weren't all that cruel here, but they could be. I went to counselling sessions too, because it was hard for me to not think of Cindy, especially because of the song I just heard. I spoke with one of the psychiatrists, one Dr Ned Nelzoni, who tried to snap me out of my torment. I found the sessions rather difficult, as if I was walking through molasses, and worse. I knew molasses could be removed; memories like mine could not.

I laid down on the long couch in Nelzoni's prim and mighty office, where doctorates of digital reminders hung on the wall, and a small dark blue curtain fluttered from incoming breezes. His plain face stared at me from a widened viewpoint.

And so, the session began. 'So Elias, how are you feeling today?'

Triggered, but undeterred, I answered softly, 'Fine.'

'Let's go back now in dealing with your late wife, where did you meet her?'

'In Anarchia,' I slurred, slightly drugged from the medicines I was given.

'What was it like to live out there? Take your time, if you wish.'

This reminded me of the trial Silage and I were in.  'Barren, forbidding, and you're a slave to the world, maybe to yourself.'

He nodded, 'I see.  Was she a troubled girl, or certain of herself.'

I thought back to the times when she showed fortitude and when she followed the fashion of wuss.  'When I knew her, she could fight off anyone.  Had a good mind and very resourceful.  However, when we went to Dracos, she had an uncontrollable fear.  Before she died, she told me she was pregnant, which I then linked to her fear and instabilities during our time there. I felt sorry for her, but there it was.'

'Was she put under any stress?'

'Not at first, but when the Draconians demanded an answer to our whereabouts in space, a gun was put to her head.  I think that would constitute stress,' I yelled, getting up.

'Easy easy, now Elias,' Nelzoni soothed me, 'Lay back down and relax.  Do you want another sedative?'

'I've had my dose already.'

'Doesn't look like it's working much here.'

'Look,' I focused solely on him, 'I've been put in a hard-core situation.  My loyalties were doubted, I have a brother that will be executed, and a wife who died.  How does that grab ya?'

'Elias, I am sure you did nothing to betray Earth, nor did you attempt to further Draconian interests.  You do care about your family. Would you like to see Silas?'

I stiffened my resolve.  'No.  There is nothing more to say to him.'

'Well, it's your loss.  The only link to family you've got.'

'The only link to family I had was killed on Dracos,' I weakly replied.

The thought of Cindy came to mind, and knowing that a former best friend had shot her, pierced me in the gills.  I got up from the couch and intended to punch out the wall, as I thought about Silage and his would-have-been treachery. *Nelzoni didn't deserve the punch.*

'No Elias,' he grabbed me, stopping me before my fist hit his precious enclosure. 'Throwing punches at walls will not do you any good.'

He held me, until I weakened my resolve.  Nelzoni then went to ex-amine his notes, and pulled out a vial with accompanying needle.

'This shall calm you down,' he said.

A needle was put in my arm, the sharp pain followed an amount of bliss I never felt before.  I had forgotten myself once again.

'Now these outbursts will have to end, Elias,' Nelzoni warned, 'You must accept your pain for what it is and heal.'

The doctor put the stinger away and led me out the door.  Someone waited for me, the gentlemen in blue, to take me back to my room for a long rest.

# CHAPTER X

Meanwhile, Silage wasn't doing any better than I. Everything he had was left behind on Dracos, in our hurried, possibly harried, flight out of there. All his precious books and magic tricks were finally lost to purpose. Whatever he remembered from them was all he had. It was too bad. The apartment where he once lived had already been prepared for the next occupant.

The books were a mere curio to the Draconians, but they did not match their ideals in life. When the books were about to be put to the flames, a passer-by made enquiries about them. He asked if he was allowed to save them from destruction. The fellow in charge agreed to the transaction, and, thinking nothing of it, the passer-by made off with Silage's old books. Despite them not believing in such notions, the books did make for fascinating reading. They could be useful in a library of what not-to-do. I guess there could be a little magic after all on the Draconian planet, wherever they now resided these days.

The trouble was that, aside from myself, he sorely missed Cindy. His minor flirtation with her was just a quick fancy, but when she was dying, he found he really loved her; as a sister, at least. There was a point where he wanted to share her with me, but I wouldn't allow for it. Much to his discomfort, his decision to remain on Dracos was what got him to this point in the first place.

He sat in his morbid cell, and closed his eyes, shutting out any activity around him. He recalled a small chant from the texts he once possessed. Drawing from their Celtic origins, he made them his own. It led him to a deeper induction of himself. He chanted away, quietly, soon developing into his own rhythm. He thought about other people in condemned cells during those ancient times, and reckoned they coped like he did, by figurative chants. It didn't matter to him about it. He just did as they did.

He knew he was in the wrong though, in *wanting* to use information against me; but in reality, he really didn't do anything. All he did was to change planets, as it were, living somewhere else, just like the Draconians did. They were from old Earth, too, but they morphed into a power-species that was about to rock the known galaxy. With his help, they might have flourished. As of now, I couldn't tell. I figured they'd get on well, knowing their luck and vast skills.

Days passed for him, as the further talks about lowering the sentence were resumed. Pemur again fought the Council bitterly, just for my brother's sake, trying to reason with Dr Ruckus. Yet, to reason with Ruckus was a stand-off, and the Council stood firm about it. The computers really hated the fact that Silage was on Dracos in the first place. They didn't like Elias Huer, Sr's choice of putting him there, just to attend 'school'. It annoyed their circuits, and wanted to be done with him immediately. But they had to follow their own rules, allowing for opposition, so Pemur won for that small moment.

It was a sad one though, because he really wanted to save whatever family I had left. He felt bad about Cindy; there was nothing he could do there. However, with Silage, still living for the time being, he had another, final go at the Council. Defeated, Pemur walked out and sent Silage the closing act of execution. It would now be mere hours before the conclusion.

Silage lay on his bunk, still chanting, hoping for a sign. He carried on for a time, relaxed in deep thought. He wasn't right, nor was he wrong. He wanted to carve a life for himself, and please his superiors. As Dracos was evolving as an entity in its own right, he thought it would be best to serve his new masters the best way he can. But this loyalty was tried, and relations between him and the Draconians soured.

The Kanes were completely at home there, and probably enjoyed themselves immensely. Silage remembered them as boys and how he was friends with Silver Kane. It all seemed like a tragic splurge into nothingness. He thought he could cope well in that society, making himself as glamorous as possible in order to accomplish it.

Now, he was considered a traitor to the Directorate, even to Earth, according to Dr Ruckus and the Computer Council. His wish to carry out his mission to find out about the stargate cost him dearly. Technically, he was no traitor. He never got a chance to reveal the stargate to the Emperor like he intended. It was a sad foray into a world that didn't really know him well.

With my visit to the Draconian moon with Cindy, it had complicated matters, but gave opportunities as well. Little did my dear brother Silage know that two could play at his own game, and I foiled the plot for him. I never regretted my actions on Dracos, ever, because I knew Silage's revelation would lead to no good. If the Draconians knew about the stargate, which I thought by now they would, the galaxy would be theirs and no one in his right mind could say any-thing about it. I tried to save it from this sort of domination, but like everything else in science, it just needed to be discovered. The star-gate was there to be discovered, be it by me, or the Draconians them-selves.

Silage didn't think he was a traitor to any cause. He got into my mind, and the information inside was given to him. Yet, it was my in-genuity that saved the day, as I had put him to sleep, preventing him from seeing the Emperor and blabbing to him about my travels. So, when I went to see him, I pandered the Emperor and revealed another story to him. Yet it was the *intention* that got everyone else and the Computer Council aroused, and who called him a traitor.

Actions taken could put you in a category, but carrying out those actions were a different thing entirely. I never thought of Silage as a traitor at all, but his attempt to serve the Draconian cause made him one. It was too bad about it, but no love lost in between. I never saw him again, being confined to my own cell at Nuconnalow. I thought about him now and again, but never wanting to be close. Silage didn't think so, either.

He laid in his bunk, still, wondering what tomorrow would hold for him. *No matter; he knew.* The executions of the 25th century were swift, but tried not to be too inhumane. If it were say, five hundred years earlier, he might have gotten away with just life imprisonment. *Not today. Not anymore.* The Computer Council under Dr Ruckus was prone to give just desserts to those who deserved them. Silage didn't need any further comfort from me, nor anyone else. He just laid there, as the lids of his eyes closed. He began to shut down, continuing his chant. An old, forgotten death chant now emerged from his lips, which he learned from one of the now-lost books of his. His focus on the words was pure and the foretaste of the ethereal hung upon him. The light which now started to sputter and fizzle was dimming, and soon he laid there in permanency.

A passing guard checked up on dear Silage. He wasn't happy with what he saw and called another guard, who approached with a key, unlocking the door. They found Silage's body lifeless and limp. They then sounded the alarm.

# CHAPTER XI

It took a week for news of Silage's death to filter down to me here at Nuconnalow. In this facility, good news, as well as the bad, took its time, due to the emotional instabilities of some of the patients that must be considered. It had been several months since I'd been at this place, and if you think I enjoyed it, think again. I felt weary at the seams, but I wouldn't go so far as to take my own life. I also didn't think Silage was a weakling, giving in to passions he didn't understand, but I wasn't surprised. Being executed at the behest of the Computer Council was nothing to sniff at, nor was it something to be proud of. I guessed that was why he took his own life. Again, not something to be proud of, nor wish to talk about with anybody.

I missed Cindy, and now I had to deal with Silage's death. *Ugh, what's a man to do?* Soon enough, an ageing Pemur, worn around his edges with grey, came up to me, as I indulged in my now favourite past-time of gardening.

'Elias,' he said, putting his hand on my shoulder.

'Please, it's alright,' I answered, carrying out my work.

'I'm petitioning the Council to free you completely. Dr Ruckus has made a huge miscarriage of justice, in light of your brother's suicide. Theo will be a good defence for you again and I think we could persuade the Council now. We all know it wasn't your fault, and though Silas's intentions were questionable, we found that he hadn't committed treason. The Council was proved incorrect, and my arguments to them paid off. You kept your discovery of the stargate a secret, and that is what matters.'

'But I am certain the Draconians found the stargate by now.'

Pemur touched his greying sideburns.  'I agree.  If they had found it by now, they did so on their *own* accord.  We did not lead them to it. That is what the Computer Council really was after.'

'Well, thank you for keeping to our cause,' I smiled, 'What is to become of Dr Ruckus?'

Pemur sat down beside me, putting his fingers in the dirt. 'He'll probably stand down and get reprogrammed into something less harsh, like Administration.  The Judiciary carries a hefty responsibility, too much for a broadened ego like Ruckus.  He protested strongly, stating he didn't want to be hanging around a quad, like his colleague Dr Theopolis. His views seemed very outdated, nearly coming from a time your brother would have loved.'

I laughed at that.  'Imagine them two together in that circumstance!'

Pemur continued, 'We decided not to destroy him or anything like that.  The circuits inside him are too valuable and thankfully reusable.  We'll just tone him down slightly.'

'Your hands are dirty,' I commented to him, seeing him play with the dirt as I had.

'Yeah, I know.  Feels good, yes?'

'I thought the other computers programmed him,' I noted.

'They did,' Pemur answered, 'That is why Ruckus turned out the way he did.  Too much perfection in computers leads to megalomaniacal results.'

I felt hopeful.  'So when will I be released from this place, and work for you?'

'As soon as you could fill a post for us,' he smiled.

'You're giving me a job, just like that, with no opposition?'

'When you're ready, willing and able.  It's a condition for getting you out of here.  I am now responsible for you for the moment, until you regain your senses. You'll be working alongside me.  As your abilities reveal themselves, you may take over.  I cannot last forever, even in these advanced times.'

'Your age is showing,' I said.

'Yeah, I know.  This is why I need you, Elias.  You are a continuation of your father's work and could be of great use to the Directorate. We're also moving you into a sleeker accommodation within the Directorate building.'

'The Widower's Pad?'

'Something like that, yes,' Pemur laughed.  'I'll see what I can do to relieve you from this place.'

He got up to leave and we shook hands.  I was very impressed in how hard he worked to free me, as long as I worked for the Directorate, under him.  I guessed it was also to allow me to attend Silage's funeral.  It felt as if a huge part of me had left, even though he wasn't always present in my life.  These last few years had proved themselves, and Silage was still the same to me.  I found him nothing special, but for his interest in the primitive and archaic.

I wanted to love him, but could not, despite being my twin brother. It's like one half of me was Cindy, with the other half being Silage. Now I was tossed out on my own and wondered where it would lead me? I dug around the dirt, in a symbolic manner. I felt the old earth feed into me, and I think I started to understand Silage's love for the primitive life. I knew he'd love to be with me here, helping out, feeling the dirt among the sands of time.

I was then lost in a reverie. I swore to myself to shut out the past entirely, and all the pain thereof could go somewhere else. I was still thinking with grinding resolve, when a young girl approached me. I looked up, and for a second, a glimmer in my heart cried, *Cindihan!* But no. It wasn't her. The image soon begat further clarity, as she headed my way, looking nothing like Cindy. She was very young, probably pre-teen. Her dark hair flowed like that of a model's and overshadowed her pale face and blue eyes. A small uniform-like dress became her, as she came nearer to me.

'Hi,' she introduced herself, 'I'm Wilma Deering, but you can call me Dizzy Dee.'

The name confused me. *I didn't think she looked dizzy at all.* 'I'm Elias Huer.'

'Son of Dr Elias Huer, Sr, I presume,' she announced.

'Yes, that's right.'

*How did she know that?*

I pressed her a little. 'Why should I call you Dizzy Dee?'

'Everyone calls me by that nickname. It suits me, as I love to hang out and drive the pilots crazy, getting into everything.'

I sniggered, 'So you want to hang out with me, then?'

'Sure. I bring joy to the needy. You are needy, so I bring you joy. I certainly would love to visit with you. I took some courses in psychology, and I got to meet and learn about real cases.'

'So I'm a real case to you? Aren't you young for this sort of work?'

'Nah, the younger you start, the better off with others you can become,' she said.

I was taken aback by her forwardness. 'Are you going to help me through this?'

'I thought I was doing it already, cures of patients don't always constitute therapy sessions, you know.' She checked her chart, 'Let's see now. Oh gosh, you recently lost your wife and brother.'

'Yes I had.'

'Were you close?'

'To my wife, yes; to my brother, it was split.'

'Between what?'

'You seem very precocious for someone your age,' I observed.

'What was it split between?'

'Whether I wanted to knock him out or not.'

She laughed. 'Rivalry between brothers, especially twins, fascinates me.'

'Try swapping minds with one, then you'll really see what it's like,' I replied, 'You know, you could go far, maybe working in the Defence Directorate or something.'

'That's what I hope for,' she explained, 'My dad and his friend Noah Cooper are going to have me trained as a pilot.'

'Oh, that sounds wonderful. Good for you, your foot's in the door already.'

'What about you? What will you do when you leave here?'

'I think I will be working for the Directorate, too,' I foretold.

'Well, good luck to you, Elias Huer.' She checked her watch. 'I'll be going on my rounds now, but I will catch up with you later, if you like.'

'Please do. I would like that very much,' I smiled at her and waved.

We exchanged our goodbyes, as she scampered off into the distant blocks of other wards. My head was shaken up by her bubbly personality. It shocked me that anyone could match Cindy's vivaciousness, but to enjoy a go-getter of a girl nearly put me in stasis. I wished deeply for her and hoped our paths would cross again.

I still caressed the dirt with a spade, planting down more seeds. I found myself thinking about her more, as she was quite formidable. Miss Deering had shown great promise in the ensuing years. Under the instructions of her mentor, Noah Cooper and her father, she became a fine star pilot. She later accepted a position at the Defence Directorate, which welcomed her with open arms. Her no-nonsense bravado shown like mine, when I was a pilot, which displayed similarity between us. I missed my old piloting days, though they weren't so long ago. Now that Cindy was in the beyond, I dare not ruin a budding friendship with gripes and groans from the past, even if Miss Deering knew about them. I wanted to be free of that, in order to move along in life and enjoy the possibilities it had to offer me.

# CHAPTER XII

Time passed, and it seemed like years; they probably were, too. I was still the widower of the 25th century. I took it in my stride but there wasn't a day that I didn't spend a thought for my Cindy. She was a beautiful, child-like entity of great want and satisfaction. The wanting and satisfaction parts that I liked to refer to, was me. She thought the world of her budding scientist-to-be and fab star pilot, maybe the universe. Too bad she never took the chance to conquer it with me; the Draconians stood to conquer it instead.

I continued to have regrets about our trip, and our intention to come home straight after our discovering the stargate, had led us both down a path that forever separated us. I truly felt dismayed about it and there was nothing I could do to bring her back. Just my memories were all I cherished.

Breathing out a heavier sigh, I thought about Pemur Oppenmach and how he got me through the current moments of my life. Before I entered Directorate life, he helped me in achieving some latter parts of education that I needed to undertake, since I'd been away so long. Once I finished, I had gotten that cherished Doctorate degree of Science and Administration. I now fashioned myself as Dr Elias Huer, just like my father. It suited me, but the deja vu resonance of it gave me the creeps.

The more difficult portions were still hard to swallow. Silage took his own life before being put down by the Computer Council; Cindy had died through Draconian hand-weaponry. There was a child inside her too, succumbing to the blast itself. So much weighted down upon me, I soon began to look older. I was not even forty years old, but I might as well have been. The past several years had taken their toll on me.

Once Pemur's intervention with the Council got me out of Nuconna-low, he had me work for him at the Directorate offices, Science Division, after the educational side-trip. It was a step up from what I had been doing, as much of my time of the past few years was spent exploring Anarchia, Arachnia, the outer reaches of the solar system, and Dracos. They were still a memory of good times; but it felt like a long time since I'd been 'home'.

Once home, though, my patterns did not fit like a glove. Without Cindy, I was lost. Without Silage, I had no one to argue with. The two people brutally removed from my life was solely too much for me. I even had more trouble sleeping, than anything else. After one of those fits of nightmarish proportion, I put my hand on the other side of the bed. The hand laid flat. The other side was empty, devoid of the living sparkle that captured my world.

For a second, I had thought the good lady would have gone off to the bathroom or something, *but no.* The night owls hooted loudly in their forests, and in my waking moments after, I realised she was no longer there. Only shadows remained, and they were extremely deceptive. I wailed, alone in the night, crying my eyes out, and hoped one of the night staff nearby could come and help me. I was all strung out, and a rewind was out of the question.

As luck would have it, Lt Selina Cayley suddenly burst into my room. 'Elias, are you okay?'

I looked at her with puppy-grim eyes; another sign of ageing. I sobbed again, 'No. '

'Maybe you were better off in Nuconnalow,' she suggested.

Dismissing the earlier weakness of tears, I braved it off. 'No, I'm fine. Really, I'm okay.'

'You sure?'

I lied to her. *I was not okay.  I was not okay with anything.* I was angry, I was hurt, I lived in a maelstrom of dirt. I deeply sighed.  If it had been an earlier era, I would have fought a duel with Antssarah Kane to gain my sanity back.  *Oooh, I would have gotten him good, if I had the chance.  Standing back, pistols forward, the great shot, and... what else is there?* I was furious with myself that I couldn't do this now.  It would be too archaic to the Council's mother-lode of electronic comparisons. *No, no duels.* Ruled out by centuries of latter better-being.  *Oh phooey, who were they kidding?* We were humans, and there was nothing the Council could do from us being the most misunderstood bunch in New Chicago.

With the Draconian's probable knowledge of the stargate, who knows what more destruction Antssarah or his people could bring?  I already foretold it in my mind what they would do.  All they want to do is have the best time, conquering other worlds. Now, all I had were bitter memories, woeful tears, with the realisation that my brother's interest in the distant past was not a good thing.  His interest in Dracos itself wasn't very hot, either.

The lieutenant called out, ' Dr Huer? Elias? '

'Yes, Selina?'

I called her first name aloud to be a nuisance.  She came up to me and hugged me.  'If you want to talk or cry, please…'

I breathed my last helpless breath.  'No need.  Thank you.'

She smiled and she left the room, leaving me in my doldrums. *Maybe I should have taken up her offer.  No, I couldn't.  I wasn't like that.  Nor was Dad.*  He never wore his shirtsleeves exposed and neither will I.  I wiped my tired eyes of the helpless tears that hosted Olympics on my face.  I had to be brave about it.

I got up and looked in the mirror.  There were some lines and creases looming, mostly around my dimples.  My once stunning looks gave way to a fiery set of gently soft-spun wrinkles.  Yes, I was ageing, but I was ageing *alone*.

I felt even worse for my brother, let alone Cindy.  I hated him for most things, but passively wanted a piece of his charming self within me, so I could be just as charming, without the boring parts.  I had the chance when I strutted bravado around Dracos, in front of the Emperor, and with those women readying themselves to be my wives. *Wow, I blew that one but good.*

Silage was a great asset to someone, no doubt, but for the wrong reasons. If only Dad made him study in New Chicago.  I was certain that there were universities taking on crazy misfits like my brother in their struggling history departments. After all, history was not a subject worth attaining, as we needed to grow beyond such values as of late.  Yet, there were those who were interested in the archaicness of it all.  It proved to be more than an impression.

But what was more scary for both of us was our being tried for treason, or at least the *attempt* at treason.  The Computer Council made it known that even intentions were as bad as the real thing. That was what they hated about human resolution.

*You could change your mind*, the small, circular micro-machinery figured. Silage did not, and had intended to tell the Draconian Emperor the knowledge of that stargate.

I figured that their Empire is half-way across that side of the galaxy at this moment, with the extreme likelihood of them being in charge of it. I hated myself for being a part of this mess and I thoroughly paid the price. My anger at the Draconians took hold of my heart, replacing it from the love I had for Cindy. They stripped me of a wife and flogged me with their proverbial chain.

The reality of loneliness seeped in, day by day, even when working for the Directorate. There hadn't been a day when I hadn't thought about it all, trying to make sense of it, if possible. Even logic could not stop the madness seeping cruelly into my prime. It was time for me to send for Dr Nelzoni's services once again.

# CHAPTER XIII

There were people in the Directorate who were trying to pull me through all the hate and horror I experienced and get me to further myself into the world Pemur offered me, through science, logic and potential discovery.  He guided me like a missile and worked with me on occasion.  From this point on, I hid myself behind my desk of science for all days.  I did socialise with people and attend Director-ate functions, which required my presence.  However, my time was best suited within the cosy confines of test-tubes and mathematics.  If you weren't careful, there were also storage jars that go boom in the night, but I never worried about that.  The only thing that went boom in the night was me.

Pemur and I discovered a newfound element in the midst of our subtle experimentations.  It was telogen.  It was like a plastic-mould compound, and he came up with the term.  It sat in a Petrie dish, looking ever so brightly, as one of us gazed upon it with a micro-scope.  Luckily, we both got to see it together, as there was an exten-sion of the eyepiece for another.  We decided to use it in machinery, and break it down to us in the circuits of newer drone models, created for a later date.

We formed a tight-knit bond of friendship, that wouldn't unsteady it-self with the simple untying of a knot, being widowers together.  He never discussed his personal life with me, as I was unaware of it in the first place.  But he knew Cindy, and she was a topic of many a conversation with him.  Pemur opened up somewhat a little, but con-fessed that he found Cindy refreshing and if it weren't for me meet-ing her, he would have liked a chance with her.  I became rather dis-turbed by this, remembering how Silage wanted Cindy too.  How-ever, I didn't let this come between us, as I already lost too much. Whomever I had now, must remain.

One day, in the lab, I made a small comment about the telogen's reproductiveness. Pemur lost his temper and shouted, 'How could you reproduce, you can't even survive!'

I tried to ignore his raucous comment, as I furthered my way into the circuit. *A little more here, a little more there.*

He put his hand on my shoulder, apologising for the gruffness, 'I'm sorry Elias. We've been here too long. Let's go out for a drink.'

'I'd like that very much,' I accepted his kind offer.

Pemur's age was hitting him hard and 'losing it' became a staple of his ever-widened personality. It showed in many different facets, like a woman's hidden charms, but there was nothing charming about age. Sometimes he was known as the 'White Owl', because of the sensitivity damage to his skin. The feelings and the wrinkles that went with age became more sinister, but not in an evil sense. I looked at him and saw his face changing as the days went by. *No different from mine.* He had a small resemblance to Dad that surprised me, which was equally disturbing.

Later on, after the comfy night of light drinking and merriment, I looked at myself in the mirror. I saw the fellow of age creep up on me, too. I put my fingers into a jar of ageing serum and tried to rid myself of the years of wear. I used the ointment to hide blemishes, wrinkles and other dark matter around me. Yet Silage willed his youth upon him, not use a quick-in-the-mud beauty treatment like a female would. I also noticed there was a slight tan on my skin. I wondered why and how. *Oh yes, that time in Nuconnalow. But wouldn't that have faded by now?*

Otherwise, I saw myself as plain as a day in Anarchia: boring, desolate, and hopeful.  Hopeful in finding someone like Cindy, which is a dream that I know will never again be exceeded in my lifetime. Some people tried and some people failed to get me back on the dating scene.  Like an old 20th century game show, I became the central magnet of attention.  What kind of attention, I couldn't say, but I doubt it would be pretty.  Even Miss Deering, who I became rather fond of recently, made various attempts to snag me up with someone who could fit my personality.

By this point, Miss Deering was a few years older, well past the youthful girl I remember visiting me at Nuconnalow.  She was nearly finishing the latter part of her education and attaining her pilot's license.  Though I knew her as a friend, I didn't want it to become more. I knew she was much younger than me, and she wasn't Cindy. Her maturity grew stronger about her and Miss Deering would make a fine catch for someone who wanted to look. *I wasn't one of them.*  I devoted my life to research and experimentation.

'You're so crusty,' she said to me.

'I cannot help what I am,' I answered, 'But I am more keen on lab rats than romance.'

'You just don't want to be hurt, that's all.'

I gulped down another tearful cry.

'Well, put your beakers aside,' Miss Deering guided me, 'We're going out.'

'Out?'

'Yes, out.  I'm going to take you to a club and you're going to enjoy yourself, even if it kills you.'

'Well, in that case, I will join Cindy,' I declared, with fond hope.

Miss Deering nearly lost her temper, like Pemur, and grabbed me. She stuffed me in her Runnabug Scout-class vehicle and blasted her way toward the inviting sunset.  The vehicle was a two seater, with a tucked away third in the back, if you took away a panel or two.  We ended up at a bar and dance hall, *Samjay's*.  People danced as the music played, they mingled among themselves over their drinks.  I could have sworn I saw something like this on Dracos with Cindy, or maybe here, I couldn't tell anymore.  Personally, my mind wasn't in me; I just went with the flow of things.  I suddenly had a hankering for the well-valued drink, *the fuquwer.*  I disregarded the notion, as I didn't believe they'd serve such a drink here. It may have gone past its prime.

I hoped I was still in my own prime, as I seemed to look decent in front of the many sparkling people around me.  The speed trap was set, as someone had followed me around, only to get an earful of science and my discovering the stargate.  That sort of small talk was handy as a light dragoon, but not here.  The person then walked off and went to dance with a more animated gentlemen.

Noticing my stiffness, Miss Deering offered me a drink. 'I'm getting one, you want?'

I blushed, knowing the type of drink that I wanted.  My face was as red as my jumpsuit with the gold trim. 'A fuquwer, please.'

When she went up to the barman Quade to order our drinks. He stared at her, and said, 'Look, I'm not up for it, lady.'

She then got quizzical.  'Up for what?'

Quade kept his steady gaze on her; the name of the drink soon dawned on her, sounding like...

'I'll… I'll go ask my friend again,' she hurried along, embarrassed.

'You do that,' the barman took his cloth and wiped the counter with it.

Miss Deering sheepishly ran back to me with a proverbial tail between her legs, and asked my request once more.

'A fuquwer, please,' I smiled.

She stood deadpan at me.  'Apparently there is no such thing.'

'Well in the Directorate, Cindy and I...,' I recalled.

'Well, Cindy is no longer here, and you are not within the Directorate's confines.  So what will it be?'

*Oh dear, our date was not going well at all.*

I recanted and suggested, 'I think I will have a smooth coffee.  Can they handle that one?'

She stared daggers at me and returned to the bar with my request.

'That friend of yours has strange tastes,' Quade said.

'He's part of another world, another generation.  He lost his wife and it was something they shared together, I guess.'

'Well, I am sorry about that, but please don't take it out on me.'

He served the drinks and went to the next customer.  Miss Deering went off to look for me, as I caught a glimpse of a young girl I thought was Cindihan.  It was a moment's notice, when I realised she was someone else.  *Kind of familiar, though.*  She smiled at me, and looked smart in her open-necked top and her hair trimmings going off the side lines.  She got keen and decided to join me.

*Where is that buckin' coffee?*

She went right for it. 'Pardon me, is this space taken?'

'No, no, I'm waiting for someone,' I grinned.

'Well, while you're waiting, let's dance together,' she suggested.

Awkwardness bespoke the moment, as I was led toward the dance floor with other party dwellers. We found a spot to dance in, as the music played quite loudly.  It did remind me of the days with my dear wife, and an ancestor of mine who also enjoyed a dance or two with his missus.

'My name's Jane Cayley, Ensign.'

I awoke to the recognition. 'You're Selina's daughter.'

'That's right,' Miss Cayley beamed, 'I just passed my tests.  I'm celebrating and ready for action in the stars.'

'Flying tests?'

'Yes.'

'Good for you,' I smiled at her, *remembering when I went off flying into the distance, with...*

Suddenly she recognised me, after a few minutes went by. 'Oh my God, you're Dr Elias Huer, the scientist.'

'That I am.  Have been for some time now,' I replied casually to her. I thought her reflexes must improve to fly those Runnabugs, a way across time from *The Ancient Crab.*

I was still wondering about that coffee I was now getting desperate for, when Miss Deering finally turned up with the sacred cup in her hand.  It was obvious she scoured the dance floor looking for me. No sooner than that, I gently took the cup from her hand and drank a bit from it.

'I see you've met the lieutenant's daughter,' Miss Deering stated.

Gulping a drop, I whispered in her ear, 'Yes, she's a chip off her mother's shoulder.  Needs to refine the skills though.  It took some time for her to realise who I am.'

'That shouldn't take long,' she smiled at me.

I still had the cup to my lips and finished it off.  Ah, how refreshing that was, the traditional coffee bean flavoured with cinnamon and vanilla.  I reckoned that was how coffee was meant to be drunk nowadays.

Miss Cayley said goodbye to me, and hoped for another dance, while reeling back to her barrage of friends waiting for her. Couldn't understand why she'd wish to dance with an old-sort like me, a scientist! *Wow, what was this world coming to?*

'I'm sorry I took so long,' Miss Deering lamented, 'Quade didn't know what a fuquwer was, and you'd walked off and I was trying to find you.  What is a fuquwer, may I ask?'

'It's a restorative, but it is not served in these type of places,' I explained. 'I just hoped someone around here, would, you know...'

'Ah, to conjure one by magic, Dr Huer? Like your twin brother,' Deering teased.

'Yeah, just like my twin...,' I trailed off, thinking Miss Deering should call me anything but Dr Huer in private, 'Call me Elias.'

'You can call me Wilma.  We have been friends for a good length of time.'

'That we have,' I agreed, remembering that ol' dirt-bed I was working on that day I met her, when she was a child. 'I do not want it any other way.  As an aside, what do you think of Miss Cayley?'

Wilma looked sternly formal.  'She is too young for you, Dr Huer.'

My face went violently crimson, projecting even deeper hues to my jumpsuit.  I remained silent. Not knowing how to answer her, she took my hand and held it comfortably. She noticed my reddened countenance. ' No cause for unease.  I was only kidding about her being too young, Elias.'

This was no surprise, but it felt like I was with Cindy again. The touch, the minor overtures, the weird suspending feelings that led to a cascade of wonderment. I looked again, and saw Wilma's white-toothed smile flashing brighter than the neon sign above this establishment. It led to the kind of moment you wish for, but this wasn't the case here. *I liked her, but nah, I just couldn't.*

Not wanting to be wasteful, I figured I'd initiate her into something more useful: stargazing.

So I asked, 'Would you like to come to the observatory with me and do some stargazing?'

Not wanting to pass up a good opportunity to see what was out there, Wilma agreed and we left the din of dance music to a quieter place, up toward the Dean Observatory, where I led her to the row of telescopes showcasing the best seat in its theatre.

# CHAPTER XIV

The stars were all out, playing with one another and looking oh-so-fascinating.  To me, this is where everything started; my love for Cindy, my brother's further interests in antiquity, and the spacial body that shot forward somewhere nearby was the Januard.  The glistening array that showed themselves as stars made it all worth it.  The Januard ship, as I now knew it as, had steered up for attention.  I recalled it in my youth, being celebrated annually, as well as in my adulthood, and being there as a first-hand glimpse on my space adventure with Cindy.  It looked just like any other star originally; long ago, we made up funny songs and aspects about it to sing on its special day.  However, close-hand experience told me otherwise; it was an antiqued ship floating in space.  *Might have done well in a junk yard sale.*

Wilma stared blankly at the Januard, not really fully understanding it, and got a pair of her own pocket binos out.  She focused them on the floating body.

'It's beautiful, but it's in the shape of a ship,' she noted.

'That's because it is a ship.  It is the same ship Cindy and I discovered way back when we found the stargate.  I wanted Pemur to arrange an exploration of it, but he declined the engagement.'

'It looks abandoned,' she dismissed, 'Not really worth anything.  Pemur would have been disappointed, if you had gone out for it.'

'I agree,' I lied, for telling her otherwise might put me at risk with the Council *again*, 'But it looks good amongst the rocks of space.  And with space comes possibilities.'

*There, my optimism, at last, shone through like a gleaming sun!*

'That it does,' she peered through the binos again, leading to another section in the sky. 'The stars are pretty tonight. With that Januard ship, or whatever it is, it makes the visuals more animated.'

I sighed and hesitated to tell her more about it, but there was really nothing I could tell. All Cindy and I saw was a ship. We don't know if it was manned or not. It looked derelict, so out of reservation and the Council's input, we never bothered with it. We didn't have time anyway, as we had our own mission to fulfil. *Gosh, if only we took the time to explore that ship, as well as the beyond of the stargate! We could have been the most valued people of New Chicago.* I could see the papers lauding us as major explorers, and we would go on many a mission for the Directorate.

Seeing the Januard made me think of the time I went through the stargate. Having passed it by once was most wasteful, indeed. *How was I supposed to know Cindy was pregnant?* The lack of knowledge and her behaviour put a damper on many things by the time we went to Dracos. It might have helped us somewhat, but women, eh, women don't tell you these things. They wait and wait, then surprise you with it when you're in a sticky situation, like we were. It was most unsettling, and led me down a more darker path in my life, which I really didn't like; full of woe and regret, and vastly expansive compared to the known universe.

Wilma then asked, 'What's the stargate like?'

*Should I tell her about it? I'll have to make it brief.* 'Well, my wife was doodling and concocting calculations, during the run in a simulator. When we flew into real space, we saw these stars that flashed and thunder-clapped as we entered. It wasn't explored fully; we took whatever data we had, and started for home.'

I paused, reflecting on the moment. 'The ship I was on, lost power and needed recharging. We landed on Dracos, and...'

Tears welled in my eyes, again. Nothing could remove this pang of grief from me; not even Julian's book, right now, could save me.

'Okay, I get it,' she held me, as I blubbered around her, 'You don't have to repeat it. I know what happened. I am deeply sorry. This is why I got you out here tonight, for distraction.'

Slightly tearful, I succumbed to weakness and continued to bawl helplessly. I felt like a child, hoping for that special treat, then being disappointed for all eternity, unless someone salvaged the situation. *No one can salvage me from widowhood.* She hugged me for awhile, knowing I was Cindihan's devoted husband; *a little too devoted*, perhaps. In my mind, nothing would take her place now, but a beaker in a laboratory.

*Yet, this lovely woman was no Cindihan Huer.* I didn't think anyone would dissuade me from pursuing Wilma. Everyone who knew me, knew I was woman-less and feeble; a mere scientist behind a desk or in a lab, playing administrator to Earth's great cause. *What was that cause?* Probably survival; feeding ourselves past the stargate to trade with new worlds, allowing alien cultures to blend with our own, enjoying Earth's hospitality.

I felt stubborn and barren without my Cindy. Even so, I reached out to her at night regardless. With hope and prayer, I would feel her body sleeping next to me, or I'd hear her flushing a toilet in the next room. Later, I gave in to curiosity, and attempted to read that Bible given to me at her funeral. With science in the forefront of my mind, I wanted to see if it was right in its approach.

Personally, I did not find it at all within the scientific scheme of things, but it was damnably comforting, when comfort was needed. In all the years I accounted for, I knew my life would be barren, cruel, hostile, and overall suck without Cindy. Even the wastelands of Anarchia had better prospects!

Life proved no real meaning for me, as I trod on my skyway, seeking a path toward another party. However, there were no parties to give to someone like me. I wasn't that old, as such, *but I certainly felt old*. The life I now was living made me feel it all the same; drudgery filled, saddened and very lonely. Yes, I had friends and colleagues in the Directorate, Wilma Deering being one of my closest. Yet, something was missing in my life; it was something I knew would never come again.

* * * * * *

It was a sunny break of day, as I gazed out my window. Twiki and Theo were with me, translating the data I'd given to them in the lab. I wasn't in the mood for the findings or endless formulations. I was in no mood for anything, really. The new year of 2491 had arrived; its celebrations, all too real. I was getting older; I was past fifty years at this point.

The Januard ship flew by once more, lending itself toward a fateful visit. I still hadn't figured out why the Directorate didn't feel the need to explore it; to see if there was someone or something aboard. *Was it a threat to us?* I didn't know. I soon regretted not doing something about it sooner, when I was in space myself with my beloved wife.

Upon a closer inspection in my viewfinder, I noted the words 'United States' that were printed one of the cells on the side of the ship, and the acronym NASA printed on the rear wing. NASA was something historical, I reckoned; one of the earliest organisations that sent those now-vintage ships into spacial orbit, a long time ago. The Januard might have been one of them. It looked intact for a ship of its age and size. I wanted to go out there so badly, I nearly stung myself over it, as tears fell from my eyes again. Remorse was a heavy price to pay, especially when you didn't have the money for it. I exhaled a heavy sigh and figured we'd have to go through another stargate to sort that one out.

I could not understand why the Council still refused to check out the ship! It was clearly one of ours, yet, it was not. This ship looked different from anything known to us in these times. The Januard was coming closer in range, but just lightly touching our sensors. *Nothing to be concerned about*, moaned the Council. They deemed it as insignificant, and no threat to us, but wouldn't it make more sense for *us* to see to its mystery? *Of course not. The Computer Council knows best, doesn't it?*

The Earth itself was recovering nicely from the Big Blast. New cities still were rebuilding after the explosion, and even extended into parts of Anarchia that were salvaged; its people, happily welcomed in. The smaller outskirts, way out in the distance was left untouched; what was left of Old Chicago was better left *untouched*. It had settled calmly into dust and no one wanted to go out there anyway.

Theo's twinkling light system on his face became lively. 'What a beautiful sunrise.'

I turned to him, thinking how odd that statement was coming from a circular unit. 'Huh?'

'He said 'what a beautiful sunrise',' Twiki repeated.

'I heard him, Twiki,' I uttered, 'I am not a total dolt.'

'Never said you were, boss.' Twiki backed down.

It was good to discourage him from such sarcasm. That wasn't something *I* taught him. Who knows what else he could learn from people?

I then addressed the circular mass of lights and circuitry, housed gently on Twiki's chest. 'Dr Theopolis, is there anything I need to know about for today?'

'Only a meeting with the Council, your experiments and Colonel Deering's patrol,' the lights responded.

*Colonel Deering. Yes. Good ol' Wilma.* All that effort putting her into flight school, and all the training provided to her, paid off. She was also part of the Directorate, and doing good service for Earth. Truthfully, I missed her younger days; the dances she took me to after Cindy died, when I returned from Dracos. She was a fresh sea breeze that really counted for something. I honestly wanted her as well, but she was... *um... young.* Not like Cindy, who would have been close to fifty by now, as I was.

My days at this point were getting a little humdrum; with all the science and maths I had studied, it continued the process. The topics were not entertaining to most people, anyway.

My free time was taken up by some reading, but all the books Dad had, which were in our childhood bedroom were gone. That Irish history and myths book went to Dracos with Silage; at this point, I hadn't a care about it. Anyway, I wouldn't know what to do with it. The book was full of misfit characters and general human pandering to imaginary gods of old. It proved to me that we were just mere cogs in a machine that usually went nowhere, be it from one century to another. Silage may have had something there, but it would not have worked out in the end.

I looked further into the sun's rising and marvelled at the enormousness of it. It consumed all the buildings with blinding neon-like light, filled with radiation, no doubt. *Not a god who threw a wobbly flash-bolt at the Earth or something!*

Theo went chattering in computer lingo with Twiki, and the responsive beading he did was getting on my nerves. I confess that I enjoyed the drones' company, which prevented me from being totally alone. That was something our society hated, as loneliness was seen as a greater disease, than the minutest microbe of bacteria excavated from anywhere in the universe.

Thinking of the sun and radiation, my mind started remembering some events that happened during my earlier days with the Directorate. There was someone I'd sent out on a mission about fifteen years ago; a fellow by the name of Cornell Traeger. Unfortunately, I couldn't recall the details of it, other than telling him the risks involved when he chose to volunteer. It had been some time since we'd heard back about this mission, and I'd wondered what became of him.

*Well, I knew what became of me.* I became a dour, sterile-minded man from the one I was, when I was younger. Wilma Deering would have been a gracious companion to me, had she been a few years older. I guess it would have been okay to court her, as we were, but I felt uncomfortable at the slightest thought of it. A situation involving a crabby guy like me, with a young and promising figure of a wo-man, who knew her place in society, would never work out.

Of course, she wasn't that young, but just *too* young for an old crust-bucket like me. Lt Cayley's daughter, too, was closer to Wilma's age than to mine. She turned her attention to being a fine pilot, and she had plenty of prospects to choose from. She went on her patrols, and occasionally stationed at the comm centre to monitor ships. She was also a good dancer, and that time I spent with her after Dracos was most refreshing, indeed. Jane Cayley proved an asset to the Director-ate and it was refreshing to see all the younger folk follow in my footsteps of flying.

# CHAPTER XV

Since coming home to New Chicago, I had gotten older, and more discreet about myself. Theo and Twiki were the best companions I ever had, next to Wilma Deering. I felt like a boy again, especially when Dad gave me Twiki for my 10th birthday. Pemur's latter-day gift of Dr Theopolis made the ambuquad complete, and both were a powerhouse to deal with. I honestly loved having the two together, though Twiki's excitable beading could get tiresome. The best thing about these guys was that they never asked any questions about my past. *Why would a 'quad worry about his master's heart?*

Speaking of Pemur, I saw him last week, just before he died. He, too, got on in years, being much older than me. I reckoned that working and being in my company must have fried his system; a true challenge, if there ever was one. There were times we had together when we laughed like mates, then fought like opponents. Our constant arguing made us go forward in discoveries, very unlike Cindy and I. Our discovery together was from a few drawings she did on the simulator, later exploring it in a ship. Pemur was a much more deeper and serious fellow. He knew I loved Cindihan deeply, and respected me for it. He never brought her up in conversation, unless I willed it.

While recalling my working with Pemur in those heady days of long ago, also I remembered when he helped in my education and I received my doctorate. I was so proud to use the Dr Huer moniker afterwards, making it a formality for me to enjoy, and others to groan at. The Computer Council thought it best for me to stay in the background for now, endlessly toiling with experimentation. I guess they had had it with me, after that trial involving Silage and the Draconians. They didn't care for my highly explosive flashings of emotion; it didn't sit well with them. Actually, nothing sat well with the Council, unless you were of a circular nature, and glared beams out as large as New Chicago itself.

In our final forays in the lab together, Pemur and I continued to work on the new element of telogen, trying to refine it for circuitry in the drones. Twiki came along to help me with the experimental model, but the unit hadn't worked. It bleeped up high minded words and trashed the immediate area, thinking it was more superior than us.

'We are computers, and can outwit you in a nano-probe,' it blurted away to itself. 'We are far greater than you.'

*If it had a tongue in its mouth, it would have blown a raspberry at us.* Thankfully, the unit's mouth consisted of a screen that lit up when vocalised. Pemur put his hand to his head, thinking what he'd done wrong to allow it to emanate such odd logic. Dispensing it for the moment, I got up and took a walk outside, with Pemur and Twiki following me.

Pemur begged me to return to the lab. 'Elias, this won't do, you just can't quit.'

'By the blood of the palate, I just did,' I huffed away in a trolley-full of exacerbation, 'Maybe this work isn't for me.'

Theo, hanging from Twiki, chimed in, 'She's gone, Elias, let it pass.'

I stretched daggers at him, as I keenly wanted to look the other way. Yet, I knew the daft drone was correct in his place, trying to make me feel better. *Damn those Christmas lights! He didn't know Cindihan Huer well at all!*

I offered Pemur, 'I'm going to the refurbisher for drink, you coming?'

'Sure, Elias.'

The day swelled in my head, after that moment. I talked with Pemur about many things, especially Cindy.  I did not know what came over me, to really expose my heart like that to him.  I guessed a fellow scientist would sympathise with such matters, especially dark matters you can see in the scope.

I was most displeased to hear that he passed away, and I cried bitterly at his funeral. I remember him working viciously with another colleague, Dr Koenig Dooson, as a last gasp of scientific work with the telogen material.  Together, they invented a sleek version of a lift, called a *tele-doo-porter*. It went in all directions, at the person's request, and it was a very fast and efficient machine.  You put on a conical-shaped, plastic ring around your head (similar to the old surgical cat collar), and you can be transported where you needed to be.  At least those experiments proved better results.

So now, it seemed my little order had left me; Cindy,  Silage, and now Pemur.  That minister, Julian was officiating at Pemur's funeral, his would-be final act.  He died a month later, and the recounting of his kindness to me after Cindy's time was unsurpassed.  It hurt me very badly how it was great to live, then lose all your friends and family at the same time, give or take a minute or a year.

I stood alone in a small room, near the lab, but not precisely in it, when I heard a voice calling out. 'Elias?  Dr Elias Huer?'

'Yes,' I turned around to see my newer friend, Wilma, who gave me possibilities in life.

'How are you?  You seem sad,' she commented.

'I'm okay,' I lied once more, hiding myself from her.  *Why did I do that?*  'No, I'm not okay.'

I broke down once more, crying.  Everything just flowed out of me. Wilma did not know what to think.  *Was I a scientist or a bawler? Could I handle the pressure of 25$^{th}$ century life without Cindy? Should I pursue another woman?*

She put her arms around me lovingly, without sin, and held me tightly; it was a grand embrace.

'Elias,' she said,  'You have log duty at 14.00. The schedule has changed, and one of other officers is taking the patrol.  You need to cover for him.'

Sniffing, grabbing a tissue from my pocket, I acknowledged her. 'Fine by me.'

'Well, clean yourself up. You cannot monitor our posts within your well of tears.  Pull yourself together, man. You're a mess!'

I never imagined I'd hear that type of mouth on her, when she grabbed a towel to make me more presentable.  A tissue was not big enough, and she tidied me up with it, like I was a mewling baby.  Yet, I accepted her chastisement, as she was correct in her findings.  *God, I'm now thinking like a scientist!!!*

My time at the log station would be spent monitoring patrolling ships going in and out of New Chicago, going as far as the stargate, and a little beyond.  Our sensors weren't that sophisticated, but not too dull either.

I wanted a bite to eat and wondered how much longer I could tolerate my given situation. I already bored myself out of my mind, imagine me doing this to others! We went to the commissary and she sat down at a table with her tray of food that she'd share with me. Engaging me in conversation, Wilma noticed my downtrodden look.

She asked me, 'Still miss her, Elias?'

I looked up from my plate. 'Who?'

She gave me a look. 'You know.'

Then it hit me, *hard*. 'Yes, I do miss little Cindihan.'

'She gave her life to protect the knowledge of the stargate from the Draconians, possibly saving Earth from invasion.'

'I know.' I tried to eat, but it wasn't working.

'You cannot ask for more. Even your twin didn't tell them about the stargate.'

'No he didn't,' I replied, 'But he intended to, as he was allied to their cause. I had to prevent that from happening, so I used his magic against him, and put on his clothing to pose as him.'

'Did he know of this?'

I recalled the details. 'We got into a fight, and I punched him out. Cindy and I put him into his bed and I used one of his spells to put him to sleep. The spell was good enough to keep him from interfering.'

'Interfering from...'

'Interfering from my plan to tell the Emperor, *something*. Being my brother, I had to act fast, so I concocted a story about my travels and he accepted it.'

'So you used magic? I guess that was better than blabbing about the stargate yourself,' she said.

'Yes, I used magic to prevent him from talking,' I stopped again, because the memory was getting heavier on my mind again.

Wilma sat there, listening to me; eager to find out more, like a hungry child. *Kind of like Cindy.*

I cleared my throat, signalling the final bit. 'I actually was thinking of telling the Emperor when news got back to him that he had a grand-daughter. Then all hell broke loose and we were sent away.'

*There, succinct to the last.* Wilma looked thoughtful, even when stuffing her face with a good meal. 'I bet they've found it by now, and are making the most of it.'

'Yes, pretending it's *their* discovery,' I lamented, 'But I felt it was good for Earth not to let them in on it. The knowledge itself proved dangerous in the wrong hands, and the intent to tell them was what got my brother into trouble. Yet, I never told them about it, neither did he.'

'What did you do then? If he wanted to tell them, couldn't he?'

'Part of the spell I put on him prevented him from saying the word *stargate*,' I grinned.

Wilma laughed about this, and patted me on the back. 'I guess there could be magic in our day and age, especially as a protection.'

'The department could be called a *protectorate*.'

We both howled at the joke when I looked at the clock and the time was nearing 14.00.

In her serious tone, Wilma ordered, 'Let's go, you've got a shift to pull.'

'Okay,' I cleaned up the table and we both left.

Together, we returned to my office, where we parted. She was due on her patrol stint, so she went to the landing platforms. I took the now proven *tele-doo-porter* to another room to monitor her, as well as other ships in the area. It was a most important task because of recent piracy in the area, as well as protecting our trading routes with other alien races; the Draconians non-withstanding, with their knowing about the stargate and their continued conquests of the known galaxies nearby.

I switched the screen on, and I had company with Twiki and his conscience and mine, Theo.

'How ya doin', boss,' Twiki greeted me.

'Fine as can be,' I patted the drone. This time, I was not lying and far more certain of myself.

I lifted the circular form of Theopolis off the hooks and put him on the table, next to the beta-screen.  Soon, there was activity.  I watched and saw many of our star-fighter ships pass by in their bulks, Wilma's being among them.

'Not much doing in this quadrant,' Twiki observed.

'No,' I stated, 'But any ships, even in the outer quadrants need to be watched.'

'I agree; we don't want anyone unofficial makin' it into our system,' Twiki answered.

'You're quite right, Twiki,' Theo said calmly 'Anything cannot get past us, without our knowledge.'

I hummed a little, focusing on something, but it disappeared in the night of space.

Somehow, it annoyed Twiki.  'Would someone check on those lights?'

The entity re-emerged in an eerie fashion, and soon, a familiar piece of machinery flew into range of the screen-scope.  It startled me, as Twiki and Theo stared at me with a curious fixation.  They then checked the screen and saw a white ship flying in the far away distance.  Their concern for me, however, was more important to them.

Theo broke the silence. 'Are you alright, Dr Huer?'

'Just a minute, just a minute.'  I turned to him, my eyes nearly bloodshot.  'Yes, I am fine, but I saw something that I remember seeing before.'

Twiki put it plainly. 'You suffering from deja vu, boss?'

I shook my head, looking at the monitor. That ship was in range and I saw it with intense clarity. I raced through my memories; the celebrations of my youth and the time of when Cindy and I first saw the Januard being a ship, not just a starry entity. The white ship flew seamlessly in space; not a care in the world could shatter its serenity. It buzzed about, seamlessly floating around on a velvet carpet.

'I, I...' I stuttered.

Both circular and human-shaped drones were even more concerned for me. Twiki chimed, 'Boss?'

I hunched backward into my chair and exclaimed, 'Oh buck!'


* * * * * *


The sky buckled under the Draconian ship, stalking the stars with unbridled ease and imperialistic purpose. The hulking, massive ship reached our space, and mingled excitedly within the system. A man with black stripes down the back of his neckline had come forth to report an exceedingly strange anomaly, fading with the patterns at the fore. Clinging to the rear of his jacket, he reported his suspicions to Silver Kane, who was in the command centre. He was astonished by the report. The anomaly was an antiquated Earth ship, just floating around like a lost particle from a grid. *What was it doing in space?* Too bad the Draconians would find out first.


THE END

48288CB00004B/1274